"Didn't first man after I left?"

"Left is the operative word. You *had* left, Alex," Shea threw at him.

"And barely a month later you married Jamie. My own cousin," he said with heavy contempt.

"Well, it's all in the past now. Jamie and I had a good marriage and—"

Alex grasped her arm. "Jamie told me how happy you were. And I died a thousand deaths over the years thinking of you with him, then hating myself because I envied him when he was just like a brother to me. I used to torture myself imagining you together, you kissing Jamie the way you used to kiss me."

Shea's mouth was dry. Her whole body wanted to move toward him, but with steely control she held herself rigidly apart.

"When you were making love with Jamie, did you ever imagine it was me?"

LYNSEY STEVENS was born in Brisbane, Queensland, and before beginning to write she was a librarian. It was in secondary school that she decided she wanted to be a writer. "Writers, I imagined," Lynsey explains, "lived such exciting lives: traveling to exotic places, making lots of money and not having to work. I have traveled. However, the taxman loves me dearly, and no one told me about typist's backache and frustrating lost words!" When she's not writing she enjoys reading and cross-stitching and she's interested in genealogy.

Lynsey Stevens writes intense, deeply emotional romances—with vibrant, believable characters. Her powerful writing style is highlighted perfectly in our FORBIDDEN! series....

In *His Cousin's Wife* Lynsey gives a moving insight into the poignancy of forbidden passion...when two people have been in love with each other for years, but circumstances keep them apart!

LYNSEY STEVENS

His Cousin's Wife

Harlequin Books

TORONTO • NEW YORK • LONDON
AMSTERDAM • PARIS • SYDNEY • HAMBURG
STOCKHOLM • ATHENS • TOKYO • MILAN
MADRID • WARSAW • BUDAPEST • AUCKLAND

ISBN 0-373-11891-0

HIS COUSIN'S WIFE

First North American Publication 1997.

Printed in U.S.A.

CHAPTER ONE

HIS strong, tanned body loomed over her, shutting out the shaft of moonlight that had been dancing between the rustling leaves above them, the light salty breeze playing along their naked bodies.

Her hands rose to touch his sleek skin, to slide over his taut buttocks, along the indentation of his spine, around his narrow hips, upwards over his firm midriff. The soft mat of fine hair on his chest curled damply about her fingers as her hands rested there for long moments before continuing their erotic expedition.

She exalted in the heady knowledge that she was exciting him, and she luxuriated in the rippling contours of the smooth flexing muscles of his shoulders and arms as he held himself poised above her.

She followed the tensed sweep of his neck, fingertips tracing the shape of his ears, the line of his square jaw, his firm chin, to settle on his full lips.

He took her fingertips into his mouth then, nibbled gently with his strong white teeth. When his lips released her, her hand went instinctively to her own mouth, tasting the dampness of him still lingering there, and then she trailed a path downwards over his chin, his throat, his chest. Her other hand, which had been delighting in the thick texture of his fairish hair, joined in again, returning to tease his small, sharp nipples.

He groaned, a low, primitive, so masculine sound that echoed in his chest, escaping to mingle with, to compliment, the murmur of the steady ebb and flow of the waves on the beach beneath them.

Then he drew a shuddering breath, his lips descending to cover hers, his body settling over her as they began to move as one...

Shea woke with a fright, clutching at the light sheet that covered her. She fought to draw air into her aching lungs as she gulped shallow breaths. Peering agitatedly into the darkness she blinked until her eyes gradually became accustomed to the night.

Her heartbeats were racing in her chest and she gazed about her, seeking and then finding the familiarity of her bedroom. It *was* her bedroom, she told herself. There was her wardrobe, her dressing table, her curtains stirring in the cooling breeze.

And this was her bed.

Yet still her hand slid tentatively sideways across the tousled sheets, feeling, seeking, and eventually relaxing just a little as she convinced herself that she was indeed alone.

The curtains shifted again and a ray of moonlight skittered across the wall, the breeze making her shiver as it touched her damp skin. Shakily she brushed back her tangled fair hair and dried her damp forehead on the sleeve of her old cotton nightshirt.

With a soft moan she rubbed at her eyes. She hadn't had that particular dream in years. Dream? She reproached herself unsteadily. No, it was definitely a nightmare, one she hadn't experienced since she'd heard he'd married.

Somehow the knowledge that he'd committed himself to someone else had seemed to lay that specific ghost, had generally allowed her to get on with her life to some extent. And over the years she'd doggedly convinced herself it was all behind her. But it appeared that this evening's disturbing events had proved her so terribly wrong.

She squinted at the glowing dial of her bedside clock: 1:00 a.m. Less than eight hours since her comfortable life had been shifted so disturbingly off its equally comfortable axis.

And yet she'd had no premonition, no inkling of what lay ahead as she parked her car in the garage and walked up the front steps. In fact she was even humming a tune she'd heard on the car radio as she deposited her briefcase in her room and continued down the hallway towards the back of the house.

'Tell me that's not the decadent odour of cooling Anzac biscuits?' she beseeched her mother-in-law as she stepped into the kitchen. The room was light and airy, filled with warmth from the large old stove and the homey aroma of baking.

'I cannot tell a lie,' laughed Norah Finlay, wiping her floury hands on her apron. 'I know how much you like them, love.'

Shea groaned. 'To which my spreading hips will attest,' she said as she sat down, reaching out for one of the still warm biscuits.

'Spreading hips indeed,' Norah scoffed. 'I don't hold with this modern fixation with being thin as a matchstick. It's not natural. A woman should look like a woman.'

'And I'm more womanly than most.' Shea took another bite of her biscuit and murmured her enjoyment. 'So much for my threatened diet.'

Norah tsked. 'Forget about dieting. You're just right the way you are, Shea Finlay, and I won't hear a word that says you're not.'

'When you're a twenty-eight-year-old matron...' Shea began, and Norah laughed aloud.

'Matron? For heaven's sake. You're an attractive young woman and I know I'm not the only one who thinks that.'

'You're prejudiced, Norah. But thanks anyway.' Shea grinned. 'Just don't tell Niall I've had one of these or he'll give me that long-suffering look of his that will quite rightly imply "do as I say, not as I do".'

Norah chuckled. 'He would at that.' The oven timer dinged and she slipped on her oven mitt, turning to open the oven door.

'Oh, no.' Shea groaned again. 'Not chocolate chip cookies, too. Have mercy, Norah.'

'These are Niall's favourites. And it's your own fault.' She glanced up at the kitchen clock. 'If you hadn't come home early I'd have had these all safely secreted away. And why *are* you home at this time? It's not like you. Or is my clock wrong?'

'No. I am early.' Shea picked up a hot cookie and juggled it until it was cool enough to hold. 'I can't believe I'm about to eat this. I can feel a kilo settling on each thigh just from the smell.'

Norah laughed again. 'So why are you playing hooky? I thought you were convinced that shop would fall down if you weren't there to hold it up.'

'Well, Debbie's more than capable of closing up so I decided I'd take extra time to have dinner, shower and get ready for the meeting tonight.' Shea pulled a face. 'So you see I'm taking your advice and slowing down. I have been a bit tired lately and I know I've been pushing myself to get this new children's range organised. So, before I get into negotiations over the new factory space, I'm giving myself this afternoon to catch my breath and relax a little.'

'And about time.' Norah slipped the used cooking trays into some soapy water to soak. 'Is this the Progress Association meeting tonight?'

'Mmmm. I suppose it will be the usual talking around in circles. I sometimes wonder why I bother to go but I suppose I should show some interest in the development of the area. I do make my living here.' Shea shrugged good-naturedly and grinned. 'I guess these meetings once a month are the price I have to pay.'

Norah laughed. 'There's that way of looking at it. But I have to agree that some of the members are a trifle long-winded.'

'You're being kind, Norah,' Shea chuckled. 'Sometimes I'm hard pressed to stay awake.'

'And is David Aston going to pick you up and take you to the meeting again?' Norah asked casually, and Shea nodded with equal nonchalance.

'Yes. He kindly offered me a lift. He sort of goes past.'

'He goes out of his way by three or four blocks,' Norah said, and added shrewdly, 'You know, I think that young man fancies you.'

'Norah!'

'Well, he does. And it's only natural. I told you before, you're a very attractive woman.'

'I'm not interested in David Aston. Or anyone else for that matter.'

Norah gave a sceptical exclamation.

'Oh, come on, Norah. David Aston's years younger than I am.'

'Two years younger and no more. That doesn't exactly qualify you as a cradle snatcher.'

'I'm not into that scene, Norah. You know that,' Shea said softly, and her mother-in-law sighed.

'It's over four years since Jamie's death, love. He was my son and I know how happy you made him. I also know he wouldn't want you to lock yourself away from life.'

'I know he wouldn't, Norah. And I'm not really doing that.' She shrugged a little wistfully. 'I just don't feel I'm ready to change that part of my life so drastically. Not yet anyway.'

'Jamie, well, we all loved him and I know he'd want to see you happy.' Norah paused. 'But Niall's growing up. Perhaps he needs a father.'

'Niall's doing all right. He has us and his teachers at school. Male and female, we're all good role models. He's OK as he is.' Shea looked up at the older woman. 'He is, isn't he, Norah?'

She nodded. 'Yes, he's a fine young man. Although my opinion may not hold water when you consider I'm his doting grandmother,' she added with a laugh, and Shea smiled.

'I do sometimes look at him and wonder if I should take the accolades for having such a bright, well-adjusted son. Or if it's just Niall's innate good sense.'

'A little of both, I'd say.' Norah began to wash her baking dishes. 'And if I was into that previous life stuff, I'd say young Niall Finlay had been here before.'

Shea picked up the tea towel and started to wipe the dishes.

'Jamie would have been so proud of him,' Norah added softly, and Shea let her gaze fall to the tray in her hands.

A tiny pain flickered in her chest, grew tentacles that clutched at her heart. 'Yes,' she agreed evenly, not meeting her mother-in-law's eyes, and they continued to work side by side, each lost in her own thoughts until the silence was broken by the slam of the front screen door.

'Gran. Mum. I'm home.'

Niall Finlay ran into the room and shrugged off his windcheater. His fair hair was standing on end and the wind had whipped colour into his cheeks.

'Wow! It was so windy down by the beach it would blow dogs off chains.' His hazel eyes widened appreciatively. 'Cookies. Excellent, Gran. Can I have one?'

Shea exchanged a glance with Norah and grimaced. 'One only,' she acquiesced guiltily. 'I don't want you to spoil your dinner.'

'No way. I could eat a horse and chase his rider,' the young boy quipped as he took a bite of his biscuit.

'I don't know where you pick up all those colourful sayings,' his mother commented and he grinned.

'From Gran.'

'So where have you been?' Norah put in quickly to change the subject.

'Riding my bike. Pete and I went down to the beach and around the place and guess what?'

His mother and his grandmother raised enquiring eyebrows.

'Someone must be going to live in the big white house around the bay.'

Shea's breath caught somewhere in her chest and she felt the warmth of colour rise in her face. For long moments she couldn't bring herself to look at the older woman. When she did, she saw the concern in Norah's eyes.

'There's a plumber's ute and an electrician's van and guys everywhere,' Niall continued. 'And they've started to paint the place. And guess what else? It's not going to be white anymore. It's sort of yellowy-cream. We won't be able to call it the big white house now.'

'That will be a pity,' his mother replied carefully, and Niall nodded.

'People are going to be all confused,' he said in a voice of doom. 'If you ask for directions around here they say, "Go down to the big white house and turn left" or "Don't go as far as the big white house" and stuff like that.'

'Yes. When you put it like that, it does sound as though we'll all have to get used to the change,' his grandmother agreed.

'Well, how about your homework,' Shea reminded her son and he went towards his room with a grumble, leaving behind a heavy silence in the kitchen.

'This doesn't mean anything,' Norah said at last as Shea kept rubbing the tea towel over the already dry cookie tray.

'No.' Shea agreed quietly.

'The big white house has only been leased for short times on two or three occasions. And Joe Rosten himself hasn't been near the place in over ten years. Why come back now? He's most likely sold it.'

'Yes, he probably has,' Shea agreed again.

'And I shouldn't think Alex would be coming back here.' Norah glanced concernedly at her daughter-in-law. 'If he had, I'm sure he'd have already called in to see us. I am his aunt. And now that his father has remarried and is living in the States he really has no ties here in Byron.'

'There's still the cottage,' Shea said absently.

'The tenants are still there,' Norah reflected with a frown. 'David hasn't mentioned anything about the cottage being on the market, has he? I mean, working for the major real estate agency in the town, David would surely know if a cottage a few doors down from our place was up for sale.'

Shea shook her head. 'No. And he hasn't said anything about the big white house changing hands, either.' She set down the cookie tray and looked at the other woman. 'Which is a little strange in itself, don't you think?'

Norah shrugged. 'Perhaps not. Maybe the new owners didn't want any publicity. And you know that's what a lot of famous people like about this area. The town closes ranks and can be as secretive and protective as a mob of minders.'

'Yes, that could be it. Perhaps a pop star or someone like that has bought the white house.' Shea relaxed a little, a ray of hope growing stronger in her heart.

'Who knows.' Norah gave a soft laugh. 'Pop stars. Movie stars. All sorts of entrepreneurs. Stranger things have happened around here, you have to admit.'

Shea smiled faintly, too. 'That they have.' She drew a deep breath. 'Well, I think I'll go and have a quick shower and then I'll come and help prepare dinner.'

Two hours later Norah called from the front room. 'Here's David now, Shea.'

Niall made a noise into his book.

'Did you say something?' Shea paused and he sighed theatrically.

'Is that David Aston again?' he asked, twisting his pencil in his hand.

'Yes. You know he usually gives me a lift to the Progress Association meetings,' she replied perfunctorily. 'Why?'

'You're not going out with him, are you? I mean, on a date or anything?'

'No. Of course not.' His mother frowned. 'What on earth makes you ask that?'

'Oh, nothing.'

'Niall, what's the problem?' Shea asked gently.

'I just don't think I'd like you and David, well, you know. I mean, he's all right I suppose but he's kind of, well, a bit of a wuss.'

'A what?' Shea raised her eyebrows at the unfamiliar term, and Niall grinned sheepishly.

'A wuss. He's wussy.'

'I haven't the faintest idea what that means, Niall,' Shea told him firmly, 'but it doesn't sound complimentary.'

'It's not that bad really, Mum. Depends how you look at it. But he is a bit of a wimp and,' Niall gazed up at her seriously, 'I guess I mean he's not good enough for you.'

'Oh.' Shea swallowed a laugh. 'Is that right? And who, in your opinion, young man, *is* good enough for your aging mother?'

Niall grinned again. 'Tom Cruise.'

Shea did laugh then. 'Mrs Tom Cruise might have something to say about that.'

'How about someone like Pete's father then?' Niall tried again. 'He takes Pete fishing and stuff.'

'A small problem there, too.' Shea pulled a face at him. 'Pete's very nice mother.'

''Spose she is pretty nice.' He sighed again. 'Gosh, Mum! Are all the good blokes taken?' he asked with his grandmother's intonation.

Shea ran a hand over his fair hair and bent to kiss him on the cheek. 'Rumour has it that that is unfortunately so,' she said with a smile. 'If I'm home late I'll see you in the morning. OK?'

'Sure. Have a good time.'

'At a meeting?' Shea grimaced sceptically. 'But, to return to the subject of good blokes, on the remote chance I do see one, I'll try not to let him get away.'

Niall chuckled and gave his mother a thumbs up sign. 'Excellent decision, Mum. See you.'

Shea was still smiling when she climbed into David's car.

'What's the joke?' he asked, and she shook her head.

'Nothing interesting,' she answered a little absently and for the first time Shea found herself really assessing him.

David Aston was quite good-looking with dark hair and eyes and he was, she knew, a relatively quiet and unassuming young man.

A wuss? A wimp? Niall's description came into her mind and she pushed it guiltily away. No, David was simply, well, somewhat dull. That didn't mean he was a wimp.

Yet one thing was certain, Shea acknowledged. She knew she wasn't attracted to him. To any man, for that matter. And hadn't been for such a long time...

Shea shifted agitatedly and quickly forced her disquieting reflections out of her mind. She made herself make pleasant conversation to distract herself from her unsettling thoughts. 'So, what do you think will be on tonight's agenda at the meeting?'

'We had a few points to discuss that were carried over from last month,' David said earnestly as he turned the car onto the road into the town centre. 'I believe I heard someone suggested picketing the council offices about the new sewerage pipes. I can't say I find that acceptable behaviour.'

Shea raised her eyebrows. 'So you're not into passive resistance?'

'Of course not. I can't see any point in making an exhibition of one's self. There are other more, well, urbane ways of doing things.'

'Mature discussion?' Shea suggested, and David brushed a hand over his dark hair.

'Of course. People do associate picketing and rallying with the, well, the unsavoury hippie element. Don't you think, Shea?'

Shea bit her lip reflectively. There were a number of alternative lifestyle groups in and around Byron Bay but Shea didn't consider them to be unsavoury. She glanced sideways at David and saw his lips were pursed in disapproval. 'I think most people would stand up and be counted if a point was to be made,' she said carefully.

'But there are proper channels. So distasteful to see all those long-haired, untidy-looking people standing about.'

Shea sighed. She really didn't have the energy or the inclination to argue with David.

'I know I'm a relative newcomer, I've only been here a year or so,' David was continuing, 'but I chose to come here because it was a quiet, beautiful little town with none of the so-called bright light attractions.'

'Well, Byron Bay certainly is that.' Shea glanced at the row of modest houses in the street as they drove past. She loved the place, with the laid-back lifestyle that was usually associated with Australian beach communities.

'I saw Niall riding his bicycle down by the beach this afternoon,' David had changed the subject.

'Bicycle-riding is one of his passions at the moment,' Shea replied thoughtfully and recalled her son's revelations about the big white house. 'How's the real estate business at the moment?' she asked as casually as she could.

'Can't complain. I sold the Martin house to Jack Percy's son. He's getting married at the end of the year and is going to renovate it in time for the wedding.'

'That's nice.' Shea took a breath. 'Niall said there were workmen at the big white house. Has that been sold?' Her voice sounded thin in her ears but David didn't seem to notice her pseudo-nonchalance.

'Not that I've heard and I'm sure I would have. Unless it was sold privately. But the sale would have had to have been made months ago for work to be legally done on the place.'

Having her suspicions verified caused a sinking feeling to invade the pit of Shea's stomach. She'd known all along that David would have been aware of any sale. And that he would have mentioned it. Businesses here were like small fraternities and they all knew how the other was fairing. A sale of the magnitude of the big white house would have set the whole town agog. Which meant only one thing—

'It's owned by an American, isn't it?' David broke into her thoughts and she nodded.

'Yes. Joe Rosten.'

'Rosten. That's him. He's the head of some big American stock-broking firm.'

'Something like that,' Shea replied carefully. 'A chain of financial advisory services. He also has a lot of other businesses. Mining. Real estate.'

'Someone told me he even had his own movie company. Is that true?'

'Yes. A small one. More of a hobby, I think.' Or a grandiose present for a much-loved only daughter, Shea added to herself, and a long dormant ache began to grow inside her. She firmly pushed her thoughts back into the dark, pain-filled recesses of her mind. She wouldn't, couldn't, allow herself to remember it all. Not now.

'Some hobby.' David turned into the parking area behind the meeting venue. 'How old is this guy? I mean, does he have a family? And how come he never spends any time at the place?'

'He has a daughter, actually,' Shea began guardedly. What would David think if she told him the whole story?

'Lucky daughter. And where can I meet her?' David laughed as he climbed out of the car and hurried around to open the passenger side door for Shea to alight.

Fortunately, at that moment they were joined by a group of people also heading into the meeting so Shea was saved trying to formulate an answer.

The hall used for the Progress Association meeting was old and draughty and the seating left a lot to be desired. However, a large crowd of people had braved the venue's shortcomings. As boring as the meetings sometimes were, quite a number of concerned citizens always turned up, Shea reflected as she took a seat beside David a few rows from the front.

Rob, the chairman, banged a glass on the table and the meet‌ ‌‌t under way. It wasn't long before the discussion ‌‌‌‌‌ down and Shea found her attention drifting.

Of course her mind went straight to Niall's revelations about the activity at the big white house. Joe Rosten, the owner and a friend of Alex's father, would be nearing seventy years old now so he'd probably be retired. Maybe he intended returning to Byron Bay? This thought of course brought other disturbing considerations. Perhaps his only daughter would be accompanying him.

And his son-in-law.

'Well, I'm not going to be involved in any protest march.' David's lowered voice drew Shea out of her reveries and she shifted in her seat, a little guilty that she had been so inattentive.

'I'm sure it won't come to that,' she began, not having a clue about the subject of David's frowning displeasure.

'Perhaps that might be a little premature,' suggested a deep voice from the back of the hall.

A tall, fair-haired man was striding towards the front, his long legs easily eating up the distance, trainer-clad feet silent on the dusty bare floorboards. He wore a pair of tight-fitting tailored blue jeans and an unadorned light sweatshirt, the sleeves pushed casually back along his forearms.

The harsh fluorescent light flashed on the gold watch on his left wrist and on the same hand, on his ring finger, he wore a gold signet ring.

All this Shea took in subconsciously. Her numbed body was apparently beyond reaction. If she had been alone and able to respond to the sound of that voice, the sight of that familiar, yet strangely unfamiliar face, she knew she would have dissolved into a shaking heap. Or simply fainted dead away. But she did neither.

Then the crowd seemed to part and their eyes met, steady coffee brown and startled sea green. And Shea's heartbeats began to race.

CHAPTER TWO

How Shea wished she could sit quietly, alone, regain some semblance of composure, away from the so public backdrop of the crowded meeting hall. In those interminable seconds she felt as though her whole life flashed before her, with all its pleasure and pain, its achievements, and what she considered her failures.

She was a young child again in Brisbane, growing up in the warmth and security of her mother's love and care. She was an orphaned twelve-year-old travelling south to Byron Bay to begin a new life with Norah Finlay, a godmother she scarcely knew. She was being thrust into the unfamiliar family circle of Norah and her son, Jamie. And Norah's nephew, Alex.

She remembered vividly the moment when she met Alex Finlay. It was etched in her mind with a clarity that easily overshadowed her arrival in the picturesque little coastal town of Byron Bay and her re-acquaintance with Norah and Jamie. And apparently her memories of her first sight of him could still unsettle her.

She had been living with Norah and her fifteen-year-old son, Jamie, for just a week when Norah's nephew arrived home from a school excursion to Canberra, the nation's capital. However, in that week of his absence Alex Finlay's reputation had preceded him.

Norah quite obviously adored him and if all Jamie said was true, then his sixteen-year-old cousin had to be some sort of god. Alex was, academically, dux of the school. Alex was outstanding on the sports field. Alex was, well, Alex was everything to everybody.

He lived, Shea was told, with his widowed father in a cottage down the road from Norah's home. Alex's father and Jamie's late father were brothers and, according to Jamie, Alex was more like a brother to him than a mere cousin.

And Shea reflected in those days before she met Alex that it was a fair indication of Jamie's character that he showed not the slightest bit of envy for this so perfect cousin.

Alex came down to visit as soon as he arrived back from Canberra. Jamie had said Alex didn't seem to get on all that well with his father. And later Shea also found Donald Finlay to be a cool, morose sort of man, certainly not the kind of person to encourage anyone to come too close to him, including his own son.

So Alex arrived.

Shea was in her room nervously preparing her text books for her first day at her new school next day when she heard the sound of welcoming voices from the living room. Moments later there was a tap on her wall and Jamie poked a smiling face around the open door to tell her Alex was here and that she must come and meet him.

And she went. Reluctantly. Not only was she basically a little shy when encountering anyone new but she was also just slightly disinclined to be meeting someone so revered by her new family. What if Alex Finlay, universally acknowledged as being so perfect, was a big-headed, arrogant, pain-in-the-neck? She supposed she'd simply have to pretend to like him, for Norah's and Jamie's sakes.

She walked into the living room behind Jamie and there he was.

His fair hair was an overly long mass of loose, unruly curls, the ends bleached white by the sun. And his eyes were dark, fringed by even darker lashes. Later she dis-

covered his eyes were brown, light tan in the bright sunlight and when he laughed, deepening to dark chocolate
when he was passionate about something. Or someone.
In that moment she knew unconsciously that his tanned,
handsome face held more than a hint of manhood.

Other frightening sensations were warring inside her.
She suddenly felt absolutely aware of herself. She was
conscious she was almost as tall as Jamie who was three
years older than she was. Her legs seemed too long, her
body too thin, her hair too nondescript. And she knew
a burning urge to be older than she was.

Alex unwound himself from the chair as Shea entered
and her legs were suddenly unaccountably rubbery. His
shoulders were square beneath his loose T-shirt, and his
faded, threadbare jeans accentuated his long legs and
narrow hips.

'Shea, this is my cousin, Alex Finlay,' Jamie said with
obvious pleasure. 'Alex, meet Shea Stanley, who's now
my unofficial sister.'

'Shea's mother and I were the best of friends since
our schooldays,' Norah was explaining. 'Even though
we lived in different states we've always kept in touch.'

As Shea's eyes moved over him, taking in each feature,
his gaze was making its own exploration of her. Until
their eyes met, held, passed an earth-shattering message.

That was the moment she'd fallen in love with him.
It had been as simple as that. They had looked at each
other and the earth had seemed to tilt vertiginously.

She could remember a multitude of incidents over the
years but that first electric moment when she was twelve
and he was a so grown up sixteen would remain vividly
in her memory till the day she died. She'd wanted to run
to him and from him all at once.

She'd also known Alex felt exactly as she did, while
Jamie's half-rueful glance had told Shea he suspected as
much as well.

So here they were sixteen years later. Face to face. And so much had happened between then and now. Between innocence and experience. But their wonderful beginning had ended on that cool autumn night eleven years ago. Eleven years. She hadn't seen him since. And now...

Her shocked gaze registered the change in him, sent the messages to that section in the deep recesses of her mind that she knew had stored away every memory of him. She could have been that same lanky child-woman if her present reaction to him was any indication. And her response to his sudden appearance filled her with overwhelming horror. She would have to admit it was a far cry from just uncomplicated surprise at his unexpected and unheralded arrival.

The noise of the meeting abated and the crowd faded into the background as their eyes met for those immeasurable seconds.

After his momentary pause he passed her, was moving up to the table at the front of the meeting, holding out his hand to Rob, the chairman.

'Rob Jones. Remember me? Alex Finlay.'

Recognition dawned on the older man and he grinned a welcome. 'Well now, Alex Finlay. After all these years. How could I forget that winning try in the footy final? We haven't won a premiership since you retired.'

A few others joined them, took turns in shaking Alex's hand, slapping him on the back, welcoming home one of the township's more successful sons.

And Shea sank slowly down onto her chair, knowing all she had feared had come to be. The very person who had taken her young life and turned it upside down had returned to up-end her ordered world. She'd hoped never to see him again.

'Who is he?' David subsided onto his seat beside her. 'Do you know him, Shea? Everyone else seems to.

Finlay?' His eyebrows went up and he turned sharply to face her. 'Not any relation, is he?'

Shea swallowed the hysterical laugh that threatened to burst from her. 'No.' She shook her head. 'No. Not really. A sort of cousin. By marriage.'

'Oh.' David continued to look at her questioningly and she swallowed to clear her dry throat.

'He was related to Jamie, my late husband.'

'I see. I take it this Alex Finlay's been away.'

'Yes. He left Byron Bay, before Jamie and I were married, actually.'

'Oh. That would be years ago. It's a wonder you recognised him if you haven't seen him since then.'

Pain twisted inside Shea, clutching at her heart. And she wasn't ready to see him tonight. Not tonight or any night.

See him! She mocked herself disparagingly. See him! She didn't have to see him. She knew exactly what he looked like, would have known him anywhere, no matter how many years came between. How could she forget? She knew every hair, every inch of firm muscle, every secret responsive...

Shea drew a deep, steadying breath. She had to stop this, stop torturing herself.

'Has he changed much?' David was asking.

'He looks a little older,' she said off-handedly.

David's smile held a hint of smugness. 'A bit longer in the tooth?'

But he's not old. Shea clamped her lips tightly closed before the words came out. He's only thirty-two. Four years older than she was. Eleven years older than he was when she last saw him. Panic rose inside her. When she last saw him. No! She wouldn't think about that. She mustn't.

'Aren't we all,' she said flatly as Rob Jones called for order and introduced Alex to the meeting.

Alex took the floor and Shea tried valiantly to concentrate on what he was saying, but the sound of his voice took painful precedence. Somewhere her mind heard him talking about deputations to the council, community petitions. Yet her other more perfidious senses clamoured for attention, wanted to luxuriate in the purely sybaritic excitement that was for Shea so atypically physical.

Various members of the crowd put questions to Alex until Rob glanced at his watch.

'Time's getting on so I think we'd better call this meeting closed. We'll advertise the date and time of the next meeting in the usual way. And in the meantime we'll take Alex's advice and I'll be carrying our continued concerns to the council meeting tomorrow night. See you all next time.'

People began to file out of the hall and Shea stood up quickly. If she hurried she'd manage to escape before Alex had a chance to approach her. Should he want to, that was, she told herself derisively.

But David was blocking her exit and for once she felt irritated by his gentlemanly consideration as he stood back to allow a group of elderly people to precede him. At long last he stepped into the aisle and turned to see that she was following him.

'Shea.'

She had barely taken two steps when the deep voice behind her saying her name stopped her dead in her tracks. It seemed Alex *did* want to approach her and she'd left leaving too long. Once again, she conceded bitterly, she'd underestimated his ability to get what he wanted.

How she wished she could ignore him, move on, leave the building and pretend she hadn't heard him, but David had already paused beside her.

'Shea,' Alex repeated, and she made herself turn slowly to face him.

She allowed her eyes to meet his again, and the pain it brought her was worse, so very much worse than she ever imagined it would be. It was an agony just to look at the long, tall, tanned length of him. He was standing so close she could have put out her hand and touched him...

How she'd loved him! And she couldn't stop some part of her reassessing him, adding the new details to her previous cache of graphic memories.

His hair, darker now, and much shorter than he used to wear it. But she remembered how thick and vital it was. She could almost feel it now. Hadn't she run her fingers through it as she pulled his mouth back to hers?

His eyes, dark lashes now shielding the expression in their deep brown depths. They'd reminded her of smooth chocolate as he gazed down at her with passionate intensity.

His features, totally masculine, square-jawed and craggy. She knew deep creases crept into his cheeks, bracketing his mouth when he laughed.

And his lips. How his lips used to drive her crazy, bring her right to the very edge of her control. And beyond. So far beyond.

Shea forced herself to concentrate on the present. Alex Finlay now.

Yes, he'd changed. He did look older. But then so did she, she knew. Any vestige of youth that had remained when she'd last seen him had gone. The harder planes of his face made him look older than his thirty-two years.

Yet it wasn't age so much, part of her reflected almost unemotionally. He had the look of a man who had been pushing himself too hard for too long. The bright light she remembered that sparkled in his brown eyes had gone, as though some inner part of him had died.

But she was being fanciful, surely. He was just as attractive, as tall, as broad, as potently masculine.

His light sweatshirt moulded his well-developed shoulders and his dark denim jeans were hugging his muscular thighs. Shea's mouth went dry and she raised her eyes guiltily from that part of his body to find his gaze resting guardedly upon her.

'How are you, Shea?' he asked softly, his deep voice playing over her like a mellow melody, so effortlessly familiar, arousing her with horrifyingly well-remembered ease.

She shrugged in acknowledgement of his polite enquiry, and she found herself fighting an impulse to pat an imaginary escaped tendril of fair hair back into her loose chignon. Speech at that moment was an impossibility as her heartbeats thundered in her dry throat.

The studied expressionlessness on his face gave her no insight into his thoughts but she just as suddenly sensed that perhaps he may not have approached her had it not been for good manners and family propriety. It would have looked strange if he didn't speak to his only cousin's wife.

And what had she expected? she asked herself angrily. Did she think he'd go down on his knees and beg forgiveness? That his eyes would burn again with that same all-consuming passion?

Fantasy, Shea Finlay, she chided. Pure fantasy. Well, his so obvious feeling of antipathy was most definitely mutual. Her stony coldness told him so.

Yet inside she was a mass of contradictory sensations.

'I had every intention of calling in to see Norah this afternoon,' Alex was continuing evenly, 'but I was held up at the house. I didn't expect you'd be here at this meeting.'

'I attend all of these meetings,' she told him with a faint lift of her firm chin, guiltily shoving aside the knowledge that her attention tonight had rarely been on the business at hand. 'I'm concerned about the future of the town.'

He nodded. 'More people should be.'

David chose that moment to cough softly beside Shea, moving closer to her, his hand going to her elbow, and Alex's eyes narrowed on the solicitous gesture.

'This is David Aston.' Shea reluctantly made the introductions. 'He works for the major real estate agency here in town. David, meet Alex Finlay.'

David released her arm and held out his hand. 'Shea tells me you're her long lost cousin.'

Alex's dark eyebrows rose imperiously as he slowly took David's extended hand. 'Cousins by marriage. We're not blood relations.'

Something in his tone made David shift self-consciously and he turned back to Shea. 'Well, shall we go?'

'I'd like to talk to you, Shea,' Alex said, pointedly ignoring the younger man, and Shea glanced irritatedly at the time.

'It's late.'

'Not too late,' he cut in determinedly. 'I'll drive you home.'

'Shea came with me,' David stated, obviously piqued by the turn of events.

'I'm sure you won't mind this time, mate.' Alex produced his practiced, disarming smile, which Shea noticed didn't quite reach his eyes. 'I want to see Norah so it seems I can save you the trouble of dropping Shea off. I go that way anyhow.'

David drew himself up to his full height, a few inches shorter than Alex, and was about to argue the point. Somehow, Shea knew he would come off second best to this older, so sure of himself Alex, and she put her hand apologetically on the young man's arm.

'It's all right, David. I'll go with Alex this time. But thank you for giving me a lift to the meeting.'

David's chin jutted belligerently but he relented and, with a curt goodnight, he reminded Shea he would be seeing her tomorrow and walked away, leaving Shea with Alex.

'Shall we go, too?' he suggested, motioning for Shea to precede him to the door and she could only do as he bade her.

Appearances must be kept, she taunted herself disparagingly as she strode through the doorway and down the loose wooden stairs. And Alex was right behind her. She could feel him with every step she took.

Shea quickened her pace, but once around the corner and into the parking lot she paused, looking about the semi-lit area for a car that Alex might be likely to be driving.

Her breathing was shallow and she made herself move forward again until she put her hand shakily on the solidness of the first car she came to, as though the familiarity of its cool metal would help her keep a hold on her composure.

His footsteps crunched loudly on the gravel as he caught up to her and her sensitised nerve endings vibrated until she could almost physically feel the touch of his body as he drew closer to her.

He hesitated then, too, and in the cacophonous silence that swelled about them Shea felt her heartbeats accelerate until the sound of them rose to almost deafen her. And then he moved around her so tense body to unlock the front passenger door for her. He stood back just as the lights of another departing vehicle flashed over them, illuminating the dark and gleaming duco of a low-slung Jaguar XJS.

Her lips twisted wryly. Alex had always wanted a Jag. It had been his teenage dream. Now he had one and his dream had become reality. It was a pity, she thought caustically, that he'd had to sell himself to get it.

As she moved jerkily forward his hand went to her elbow in an unconscious gesture of assistance. That fleeting touch burned Shea's skin and she drew a quivering breath as she all but fell into the seat in her haste to break that scorching contact. And then he was striding around the front of the car to slide into the driver's seat beside her.

Moistening her dry lips with her tongue tip Shea admonished herself as the silence screamed. Say something! Anything! She had to make an effort at mundane conversation, not sit there like a stuffed dummy. She had to show him how little his return meant to her. She had to be cool, civilised, unperturbed.

Unperturbed? She bit back a laugh. Somehow she didn't think a racing pulse, a tightness in the chest and paralysed vocal chords were exactly the most common signs of composure.

It was a caustic, unpalatable pill to have to swallow, that Alex Finlay still had the power after all these years, after all he'd done to her, to scatter those hard-won remnants of self-possession to the four winds.

And Alex seemed just as loathe to make an attempt at conversation. Glancing sideways at him Shea was unable to read anything into his shadowed features. The tilt of his chin, the line of his square jaw, only brought back aching memories and her fingers balled into fists, nails biting into her palms.

The heavy seconds stretched into a couple of interminable minutes that seemed like hours and the silence grew impossibly heavier. Now Shea felt instinctively that he was watching her. The electric tension sparked between them, flaming, growing, until Shea thought she could bear it no longer. Then he spoke.

CHAPTER THREE

'HOW'VE you been, Shea?' he asked huskily.

How did he think she'd been? she wanted to scream at him. Did he imagine a broken heart was fatal? Did he think she'd fallen apart, so far apart that she'd never be able to pick up the pieces? Well, she hadn't. She very nearly had. But the pieces had been back in place long ago, super-glued, and she'd never let anyone do what he did to her again. Not ever.

'I'm fine.' She shrugged, her voice only slightly constricted.

'You look,' Alex paused, 'great,' he finished and Shea thought she sensed a tightness in his deep voice.

She must have been mistaken, she decided, for if she wasn't— Shea swallowed quickly, cutting off the entry into that small part inside her that she suspected would begin to tremble with excitement, would threaten to race madly, wildly away. No. She had to keep herself under firm control and not allow the fascination of the old Alex Finlay to tempt her.

'Thank you,' she replied tritely, and continued when she realised her voice sounded almost steady. 'Let's just say the years seem to have been kind to both of us.'

Alex made no comment on that but Shea noticed his hands clenched on the steering wheel for a moment before he reached out to switch on the ignition. He put the Jag into gear and pulled out of the parking lot, the scrunching of the gravel beneath the wide tyres easily drowning out the low purr of the engine.

'So, what are you doing these days?' he asked as they turned onto the bitumen roadway. 'My father told me you own your own business.'

'Yes.' The monosyllable sounded harsh and she took a quick, steadying breath. She had to be cool. Aloof. He meant nothing to her anymore. 'Yes, I have my own fashion boutique.'

They were being so very civilised. Shea barely suppressed a bitter laugh. Good manners were reflected in polite conversation. They'd both been well taught.

'I design and make my own range of clothing,' she added with continued decorum.

'I can't say I'm surprised. You always were interested in that sort of thing.'

No! a voice inside her threw at him angrily. Don't talk about always. Don't dare talk about that. He, of all people, had no right to do that.

She clutched at her slipping composure and fixed her gaze on the dark outlines of the trees beyond the road, not really seeing their shadowy shapes. But the murkiness of night seemed synonymous with what had happened back then.

Silence extended between them again and Alex sighed. Shea was unable to prevent herself from looking at him then and, for fleeting seconds before his attention returned to the road, his eyes met and held hers in the semi-dark cocoon of the car's cabin.

'How's your business going? Are you doing well?' he asked and she had to consciously drag her concentration back to the theme of their conversation.

'Quite well,' she replied, suppressing the urge to tell him she had succeeded beyond her wildest dreams, that her business last year had trebled, that this year she'd extended her premises and, with the new children's range under way, she'd definitely need to relocate her factory into larger space.

'Where's your shop?' Alex was asking.

'Where the old café used to be, up from the pub on the corner. The shop next door recently became vacant so I extended and combined the two.' Her voice died away.

'Have you been there long?'

'About eight years. I started out on a small scale working from home, then tried the markets. Luckily it's gone ahead from there.'

Why was she telling him all this when she had no desire whatsoever to inform or impress him?

'Are you still working for the Rosten Group?' After a moment's pause her question seemed to escape of its own volition and Alex hesitated, too, before replying.

'In absentia. I do some freelance work for the company now and then. But I've taken a break from the full time rat race,' he finished and a heavy silence fell between them until he swung the car into the driveway of Shea's house.

She barely suppressed a sigh of relief that she could at last escape. 'Thank you for bringing me home,' she began but Alex was already out of the car and striding around to open the passenger side door for her. She climbed out and repeated her thanks.

'No worries,' he replied lightly.

'Well, I'll say goodnight.' Shea started walking towards the front door only to pause when she realised Alex had joined her. She gazed inquiringly at him and in the glow from the outside light Norah had left on for her, she saw him grimace slightly.

'I told you I wanted to see Norah,' he said, and Shea stood her ground.

'It's late. Norah's most probably in bed,' she began, and Alex held his wristwatch to the light.

'Norah in bed at this hour? I seem to remember she never used to go to bed before midnight.'

He was right, but Shea wasn't inclined to tell him so. 'Wouldn't it be better if you came back in the morning?'

'Better for whom?' he asked softly. 'For Norah? Or for you?'

'I—' Shea swallowed. 'I really don't know what you mean,' she got out, and Alex continued to hold her gaze.

'I think you do, Shea. Something tells me you aren't that pleased to see me.'

'Should I be?' The words slipped out before she could draw them back and she made herself continue to the foot of the stairs. 'Eleven years is a long time. People change,' she said as she retreated.

'They do that.' The edge to his voice made her step falter. 'But it doesn't necessarily take eleven years,' he added flatly.

Shea stopped then, her hand going to the railing to steady herself, and she heard him sigh.

'Look, Shea, we used to be friends. Can't we simply try to be that again?'

His deep voice struck more raw and tender chords. 'Can't we try to be friends?' Didn't he realise each word was a sabre thrust opening old wounds that had taken years to heal?

'Friends?' Shea bit off a sharp incredulous laugh as she turned back to face him.

'Would that be so difficult?' His eyes burned into hers across the few feet separating them and then he ran a strong hand through his fair hair.

And Shea's eyes were drawn to the movement, to the line of his forearm, the long sensitive fingers enmeshed in thick strands of hair. Almost mesmerised, she watched as he then shoved his hands into the pockets of his jeans, drawing the material tautly across his thighs, and she felt her stomach lurch in that old familiar way.

For all those long years that section of her emotions had lain dormant. No man since had stirred her in that purely physical way. Not even Jamie.

No! Not again! She wouldn't allow him, or any other man, to have such a hold on her again. Physically or emotionally.

Yet her blood raced through her veins, her traitorous senses paying no heed.

'I'd have thought we could both act like rational adults after all these years,' Alex was saying.

Rational adults? Shea clutched at her composure and her chin rose. Did he really think their ages had anything to do with it? If they were seventy she'd still feel the same. It was called betrayal.

'Look, Shea—' Alex stopped and sighed. 'OK, let's leave it that you're not overjoyed by my return. Although why—' He made an irritated movement with his hand. 'No matter. The fact remains that I am here and I plan to stay here for some time.'

Shea's heart twisted painfully. Well, she told herself brutally, if she'd been subconsciously harbouring any illusions about this being a flying visit home he had just nipped them in the bud. She'd simply have to get used to having him turn up now and then. She'd have to steel herself. And her heart. Especially her heart. Because she knew if she let him get close to her and he ran true to form, she'd never survive it all the second time around.

'We're pretty much family,' he continued with a shrug. 'We'll have to see each other occasionally.'

'I'm sure we can manage to keep those occasions to a minimum,' she said with an evenness she was proud of. 'You'll be working, I take it, and so will I. If we're careful we needn't see each other at all.' She made herself hold his gaze and his jaw tightened as his eyes narrowed.

'I'd prefer not to orchestrate any sidestepping. I think we should just behave as normally as possible.'

Shea could almost laugh at that. Normally? What did he mean? 'Normal' for Alex and herself had been spending every moment together, talking, laughing, making love. However, as she was trying to decide how to answer his comment, Norah called from the hallway.

'Is that you, Shea?'

'Yes. It's me,' she said and climbed the remaining stairs to the door. But Alex was there before her.

'And she's brought a guest,' he said into the opening.

'Alex!' Norah's hand went to her throat in surprise. She shot a quick, startled look at Shea.

'Hello, Norah,' Alex replied with a faint touch of uncharacteristic reticence in his deep voice.

Then Norah's eyes crinkled at the corners as she smiled. 'Alex,' she repeated softly, a catch in her voice, and she opened her arms welcomingly.

Alex stepped into them, lifted her off the ground and swung her around before setting her back on her feet. 'I wondered if you'd recognise me after all this time. Or if you'd want to.'

'As if I wouldn't,' she admonished him. 'And I've known you too many years to forget your face now.' Norah patted his cheek and looked into his eyes. 'But, Alex. You've changed.'

'That's to be expected, isn't it?' Alex gave a soft laugh. 'But I hope that frown doesn't mean you think I've changed for the worse, does it?'

'Of course not. Those looks of yours would still charm birds out of trees.'

Alex's grin widened, the creases bracketing his mouth deepening, and Shea felt her own mouth tighten in disgust. Norah couldn't have spoken truer words. Other girls had succumbed, she knew. But she had been the one who'd fallen the hardest.

'I'm relieved to hear it,' Alex joked, 'because you never know when you'll need a few birds to come out of the trees.'

Norah and Alex laughed easily and somehow they had gravitated into the hallway, moving naturally towards the kitchen instead of the living room where they would normally take a guest. But Alex was family, so they went into the kitchen. As though he'd never been away, Shea thought with a stab of irritation.

Norah subsided into her favourite chair and Alex looked at Shea, obviously waiting for her to be seated before he himself sat down.

'I think I'll make some coffee, shall I?' she asked quickly, hovering just inside the doorway.

'To tell you the truth I've been dying for a cup of true Finlay coffee,' Alex said amiably. 'Haven't tasted one as good since I left.'

'I'd just brewed a fresh pot.' Norah made to get up again but Shea motioned for her to remain where she was.

'No. You stay there and talk to Alex. I'll get it.' Shea crossed to the old-fashioned dresser, busying herself taking Norah's fine china mugs from their decorative hooks.

But she couldn't prevent her eyes from slipping across to Alex as he seated himself at the scrubbed wooden table. She experienced a stabbing pain at the completely natural way Alex had drawn up that particular chair. He'd done so for as long as Shea could remember.

Until he left. Her lips tightened. She couldn't forget that. He had betrayed them. Betrayed her.

She tried not to listen as Norah inquired about Alex's flight home, then about his father and stepmother. She couldn't stay and listen to Alex's easy tone when she wanted to lash out at him, fling over him some of the anger and pain that burned inside her.

Automatically she set their mugs of coffee on the table, adding the sugar bowl and the milk jug, along with a plate of Norah's freshly made cookies. Alex used to love them, too...

'Aren't you going to sit down, Shea?' His words broke in on her unsettling thoughts and she moved forward to disguise the start of surprise his voice had caused her.

'Yes. Of course. But if you'll both excuse me for a moment. I'll just, um, the bathroom,' she muttered disjointedly and made her escape. Once she'd reached the safety of the hallway her step faltered, and she gulped shallow, calming breaths.

'I'm sorry I haven't managed to get home sooner,' Shea heard Alex say and her hand went to the wall to steady herself. 'Once Dad moved to the States I lost all contact apart from an occasional note from Jamie.'

'Jamie wrote to you? I never knew that.' Shea heard Norah say and her own lips tightened. Well, she, Shea, hadn't known, either, and she felt a numbed surprise that Jamie had deceived her.

'About the funeral, Norah,' Alex was continuing. 'I got the message you left about the accident and I was about to fly home but,' he paused, 'something came up.'

Shea didn't stay to hear any more. She made herself hurry towards the bathroom.

So something had come up to prevent him attending Jamie's funeral, Jamie who had been more than a brother to him. Some business deal no doubt, she thought bitterly. How could she think it would have been any other way? Alex hadn't changed. He had been interested only in himself eleven years ago and he was still the same. Alex-oriented. Something she would never be again.

She automatically splashed her face and towelled it dry. Her reflection, face devoid of makeup, gazed back at her from the mirror above the vanity basin, and her frown deepened.

She rubbed at the slight indentation between her eyes. She looked— Well, she looked every bit of her twenty-eight years, and then some. She was definitely no longer the fresh-faced teenager Alex had left behind. He couldn't help but notice the difference in her.

Shea shifted agitatedly, hanging up the towel and grasping her hairbrush. Did it matter what Alex Finlay thought? she asked herself derisively.

Her fingers loosened the knot of fair hair at the back of her head and she raked the brush through the tangles. Then she rewound it into its confining bob and rubbed at her throbbing temples.

There was nothing now to keep her from rejoining her mother-in-law and their guest so she walked back along the hallway. However, she hesitated again before she reached the kitchen doorway as she heard Norah's words.

'And is Patti with you?'

'No.' Shea thought she heard Alex sigh. 'Patti and I aren't together anymore. We divorced. It just didn't work out.'

'I'm sorry to hear that, Alex,' Norah said softly as Shea's entire body seemed to stiffen at Alex's bombshell.

A tiny flicker of hope caught Shea unawares and she berated herself derisively.

'We should never have married, Patti and I,' Alex was saying.

'That's easy to say with hindsight,' Norah put in sympathetically.

'I suppose so,' Alex agreed tiredly.

Realising she had been holding her breath Shea made herself exhale as her chest tightened painfully.

'Our marriage lasted barely a year. We were finally divorced a couple of years ago and Patti's remarried.

She seems happy enough now.' The chair creaked as Alex moved. 'That's the way things go sometimes.'

'I suppose sometimes they do,' Norah commiserated. 'But I think it's sad when young marriages break up. There seems to be so much of it these days.'

Alex made a noncommittal remark as Norah continued to decry the modern phenomena and Shea tried to analyse her own feelings at Alex's revelation.

So Alex's and Patti's marriage hadn't lasted. Shea could recall quite vividly the devastation she'd experienced when Alex's father had told her of his son's engagement to Joe Rosten's daughter. And the pain of having to pretend to everyone that it meant nothing to her, for she had supposedly been a happily married woman herself at the time.

Donald Finlay had left for the States to attend his son's wedding and when he eventually returned to Byron Bay he had packed up his belongings, rented out his cottage, and gone back to the States to marry a widow he'd met at the wedding. Shea had had no news of either Donald or Alex since that time. Neither Norah nor Jamie had spoken of them.

A tiny spark remaining inside Shea had died knowing Alex was married and only Jamie had known how badly the news of his cousin's marriage had affected her.

Poor Jamie. He'd consoled her, knowing she could never feel for him what she had felt for his taller, smarter, more handsome cousin. Even though she'd tried so desperately for the six years of their marriage to do just that.

All things considered, she felt she could have been forgiven for feeling some delight at learning that Alex and Patti had parted. But she simply felt desensitised. Well, she could care less if Alex was married or single, she told herself and with a major clasp at her composure, Shea made herself re-enter the kitchen.

Alex immediately stood up and passed her her mug of coffee as she sat down on the opposite side of the table, as far from Alex as she could. But that was a strategic error, for now she only had to raise her eyes to look at him.

'Coffee's not cold, is it, love?' Norah smiled at Shea and she shook her head, determinedly taking a placating sip.

She glanced across the rim of her coffee cup to find Alex's hooded eyes resting on her and she stilled, her fingers tightening around the handle.

With precision timing the telephone jangled and Shea was hard put not to slosh her coffee into her lap.

'I'll get it.' Norah was up and out the door before Shea or Alex could make a move.

And with Norah's departure the tension recharged between them. Their eyes meshed and neither seemed able to break the hold.

How long they sat like that she couldn't have told but she thought she saw a pulse beating erratically in Alex's smoothly shaven jaw line. And was that his pain or simply a reflection of her own in the glittering darkness of his eyes?

Deep inside her she knew what she really wanted. She wanted, needed, yearned to throw herself into his strong arms, have his body mould itself to hers. She could almost feel him, smell the male scent of him, hear the murmur of the sea on the sand below them, see the moonlight dancing on their damp bodies.

Yes, she'd loved him then. Yet when she'd needed him most he had left her.

She dragged her gaze from his. Why, Alex? Why did you do it? Why did you leave me? The words echoed so loudly inside her head she thought she must have voiced them and she glanced quickly back at him. But he showed no sign that she had spoken.

His expression was guarded now, making him seem somewhat detached, light-years away from the Alex she had known so well, loved with such intensity and innocence.

Perhaps she had even imagined that earlier momentary fire. But her imagination wasn't to blame for the remembered feel of him, the remembered taste of him...

Her hunger was a physical pain and she lowered her lashes in case he saw just how vulnerable to his nearness she really was. When she raised her eyes he had leaned forward in his chair and an entirely different anguish caught her, for all dispassion had left his face.

'Shea!'

Her name seemed to be torn raggedly from him and his hand moved towards her. Shea felt herself drawn capriciously forward, only to check as Norah rejoined them, her quick glance going from her daughter-in-law to her nephew.

Shea hoped the telltale colour that had flooded her pale cheeks wouldn't betray her previous lapse in control. Her nerves were jangling like mechanical puppets gone mad. If Norah hadn't interrupted them Alex would have...

Would have what? she asked herself bitterly. Touched her? Kissed her? No! Never again. She couldn't, wouldn't, be able to bear it.

'It was David,' Norah said. 'On the phone,' she added, seeing the blank looks on both Shea's and Alex's faces. 'He was just checking to see Shea got home all right.'

'Oh.' Shea swallowed. 'That was thoughtful of him.'

'Yes. Very thoughtful,' Alex agreed drily, and Norah smiled.

'It's so kind of him to drive Shea to the meetings. David's a pleasant young man.' Norah beamed and Alex's smile barely shadowed the corners of his mouth.

'I'm sure he is,' he said evenly, but before Norah could extol David Aston's virtues any further a sound at the doorway drew their attention.

CHAPTER FOUR

'Mum? Gran? What's going on?' Niall's pyjama-clad body leant against the door jamb, fists rubbing at his sleepy eyes.

Panic gathered in a tight ball in Shea's chest and she stood up, taking a couple of steps towards Niall, trying to put herself between Alex and her son. 'It's all right, love. Go on back to bed.'

But by now Niall was fully awake and he came forward to stand beside his mother.

'You're Cousin Alex, aren't you?' he said, obvious excitement in his young voice. 'I've seen stacks of photos of you with my dad.'

Alex had pushed himself to his feet, too, and his expression was shadowed by his lashes as he looked down at Niall. Then he seemed to make himself relax and came around the table. 'I am Alex. But you're far too old to be young Niall,' he teased with mock incredulity, and Niall grinned.

'I'm ten,' he said proudly.

'Your father wrote to me about you,' Alex continued, and Shea drew a sharp breath.

She had no idea Jamie had ever contacted his cousin to inform him of Niall's birth. Another instance of Jamie's secret letters. She reached out and clasped Niall's thin shoulders, fighting an urge to push her son behind her, shield him with her body.

'This is my son,' she said unnecessarily, her slightly sharp voice betraying her total turmoil.

Niall slid a quick glance up at her before turning back to Alex. 'I'm Niall James Alexander Finlay,' he stated with a beam and, with obvious importance, took Alex's outstretched hand. 'The James is for my father and my grandfather and the Alexander is after you.' His grin broadened. 'The Niall bit's just mine.'

Alex laughed easily and ran a hand over Niall's tousled hair.

'Do you think I look like you and Dad?' Niall continued. 'Gran says you could hardly tell you and Dad apart when you were boys and I'm supposed to look like him.'

'You and Jamie did look like brothers when you were small,' Norah put in quickly, not meeting her daughter-in-law's eyes. 'And Niall has the same colouring. But I can see a lot of Shea in him, too.' With uncharacteristic nervousness her fingers played with the cord of her robe. 'But I'm babbling. Would you like a glass of milk, Niall? And how about another cup of coffee, Alex?'

'It's a little late, Norah,' Shea said, her hands still holding her son. 'I'm sure Alex wants to get home.'

'No. Unless it's too late for you?' He raised dark brows at his aunt who shook her head.

'Did you know my dad died?' Niall asked and Alex nodded solemnly. 'He swam out to rescue a board rider and just when they were nearly safe a big wave picked up the board and knocked Dad out and he got drowned. He was a hero.'

'He was that,' Alex agreed.

'So how come you haven't been back home in so long, Cousin Alex?' Niall asked then, as he sat down beside his mother who had reluctantly subsided into her chair.

Shea's back stiffened and she swallowed, grasping the plate of Norah's homemade cookies and offering them to Alex in an effort to disguise the inner chaos she suspected was visible on her face.

'Call me Alex, Niall,' Alex was saying. 'And as to why I've stayed away so long, well, things just seemed to work out that way.'

Shea's mouth was dry now. She could feel Alex's eyes on her and a shiver raced along the length of her spine.

'I've been fairly involved with my job and I guess the years simply slipped away from me.'

Norah set down a glass of milk in front of her grandson. 'And how long will you be staying, Alex?'

It was a question Shea knew Norah had been burning to ask since Alex had reappeared. It had, after all, been one of the first querying thoughts to seep into her own numbed mind.

Alex's gaze met Shea's, held it. 'How long am I staying? As I told Shea earlier, pretty well indefinitely at this stage,' he said levelly before shifting his attention back to Norah. 'I bought Joe's house from him some time ago and I'm doing it up. When it's finished I'll decide whether or not to continue living there or to sell it.'

'Niall said there was some activity at the big white house,' Norah commented and Niall turned to Alex in surprise.

'The big white house? You own the big white house? Mum didn't tell me that. Wow! What a mansion. Can I come and see inside it some time?' he asked eagerly.

'Niall—' Shea began to chastise him but Alex cut in.

'Sure you can. The interior's something of a mausoleum. But I'm attempting to bring some normality to the decor.'

'What's a mausoleum?' Niall frowned and Alex gave a laugh.

'In this case, sort of dark and dingy. Looks like it should have cobwebs all over the furniture and bats flapping around the ceilings.'

'Unreal! Pete and I would love to see it,' Niall said
with feeling, and then added, 'Pete's my best mate. I'd
have to bring him, too. If I didn't he'd be as mad as a
hornet.'

'Sure, Pete can come, too. Any time,' Alex told him
easily.

'When? Tomorrow after school?' Niall pressed, and
Shea moved the cookies from his reach. He'd used the
cover of adult conversation to eat two already.

'We'll see, Niall,' she warned him with a glance. 'Alex
will be busy with his renovations.'

When Niall would have protested, Norah interrupted.
'Fancy you and Shea running into each other at the
Progress Association meeting. And Shea almost didn't
go tonight.'

How Shea wished now that she had stayed home. It
would have given her more time to prepare— But she
still would have speculated about the big white house,
would have wondered anxiously if Alex might have
returned.

'Must have been fate,' Alex said easily, and Shea refused to meet his eye.

Norah laughed and Shea picked up Niall's empty glass
and her mug and began to rinse them at the sink. Maybe
that would give Alex the hint that it was time to leave.
When she turned back to the table she saw to her horror
that the older woman was topping up Alex's coffee.
However, when Norah passed him the sugar bowl he
shook his head.

'You used to have two or three spoonfuls of sugar in
your coffee,' she remarked, and Alex patted his flat
midriff.

'Have to watch my weight. Part and parcel of sitting
behind a desk pen-pushing.'

'You sound as bad as Shea. And as I was only telling
her this afternoon, I just can't understand this fixation

with weight. You look perfectly fine to me. Both of you. Shea doesn't need to diet, either. No man wants to cuddle a bag of bones.'

Alex's eyes turned to run over Shea's body as she stood by the sink. And it was as though he touched her. Touched her long legs. Touched her rounded hips. Touched her full breasts. And had she imagined his gaze had lingered on her lips?

No! She forced herself to remain where she was, across the kitchen, as far away from Alex's disturbing presence as she could get. Yet her nipples strained against the thin cotton of her blouse and she clasped both hands around the tea towel as she concentrated on getting her composure back.

'You're right there, Norah,' Alex agreed evenly.

'Bags of bones rattle,' Niall put in, his eyes dancing, and a delighted chuckle escaped from him. 'And bags of bones are sharp and pointy.'

Alex laughed with him and they looked so much alike at that moment that Shea almost moaned at the pain that clutched her heart.

'Niall has the same weird sense of humour you always had, Alex,' Norah said and then seemed to flush. 'Jamie did, too,' she added quickly.

'Alex?' Niall reclaimed Alex's attention. 'When you were in the States, did you go to Disneyland?'

'Yes. A couple of times.'

'Wow! Excellent. And do you have any kids? To take to Disneyland, I mean.'

'No,' Alex replied softly and Shea's gaze swung to meet his across the room. 'My wife and I never had any children.'

'Oh. You're married then?' Niall persisted and Alex shook his head.

'My wife and I are divorced.'

'You are?' Niall positively beamed. 'Then you'll be looking for a new one.'

'Niall!' Shea admonished as Norah hid a smile.

'What, Mum?' Niall gave his mother a look of feigned innocence. 'I just meant that while I'm looking for someone for you I can keep an eye out for someone for Alex.'

Alex laughed. 'Do you fancy yourself as a matchmaker?'

Niall shrugged. 'There's not much to work with around here but—' His gaze went with obvious speculation from his mother to Alex and back again. 'But I'll do my best,' he finished quickly as he intercepted a warning look from Shea.

She made a mental note to have an in-depth and meaningful conversation with her son at the earliest possible moment.

'I think it's time you went back to bed, Niall,' she said firmly. 'You have to go to school tomorrow.'

'Oh, but Mum,' Niall grumbled. 'I want to stay and talk to Alex.'

'I have to be off now anyway,' Alex put in quickly. 'We can talk some more some other time.'

'You said you'd be staying in Byron indefinitely. Does that mean for a long time?' Niall asked him and Shea reflected wryly that how long Alex intended to stay must be the night's most often asked question. Yet she knew they weren't unanimous when it came to the desired answer.

'I've pretty well decided to stay.'

'Excellent.' Niall slid from the chair and grinned at his mother. 'Isn't that great, Mum?'

'Wonderful,' Shea managed and returned Niall's hug.

'See you later, Alex. I'm glad you've come back,' Niall threw over his shoulder and as Shea's gaze met Alex's she saw another flash of pain cross his face before he pushed himself to his feet.

Shea followed her son down the hallway to his room, tucking the sheets around him after he climbed into bed.

'Wow! Imagine Alex coming back,' Niall said happily. 'He looks a lot like Dad, doesn't he?'

Shea nodded, swallowing the sudden lump that rose in her throat at Niall's ingenuous acceptance of Alex's return.

Perhaps Niall missed having a father figure far more than she'd thought he did. But the thought of Alex stepping so easily into that role filled her with distressingly diverse emotions. Yet she supposed it was only natural, she told herself, and glanced sharply at her son when he sighed.

'Seeing Alex makes you realise how much you miss Dad, doesn't it?' he asked softly and Shea brushed his fair hair back from his forehead.

'Yes, it does,' she said honestly.

'Do you think Alex might tell me some stories about when they were young? Dad always told me about that. Like when Dad and Alex wagged school and went down the street and Gran just happened to come along and catch them.' Niall chuckled. 'They were great stories.'

Shea felt another pang of resentment. Jamie certainly hadn't told Niall the stories when she was around. It seemed there were more secrets that had been kept from her.

An irrational anger towards Alex surged inside her. It was all his fault. He'd turned all their lives upside-down.

'I'm really glad Alex has come home, aren't you, Mum?' Niall's sleepy voice broke into her searing thoughts and she made a non-committal sound as she crossed the room, turning to smile at him before she switched off his light.

Damn Alex! Her anger resurfaced as she stepped into the hall. Why did he have to come back and upset them all? She frowned resentfully as she returned to the kitchen in time to see Alex put his arm around Norah's shoulders and give her a squeeze. He was obviously leaving at last.

'Where are you staying, Alex?' Norah was asking him. 'You know you're welcome to come here.'

Shea slid a startled glance at her mother-in-law but Norah was looking at Alex.

'Thanks all the same, Norah. I've made a couple of rooms at the house habitable so I'm quite comfortable there.'

'As long as you're all right. And don't you forget to call once in a while.' Norah began picking up the coffee mugs. 'Will you see Alex out, Shea, while I do this?'

Alex's eyes challenged her and Shea's gaze was the first to fall.

'Of course,' she said evenly and started along the hallway with Alex following closely behind her.

And she felt his every step. Her trembling fingers almost clutched at the doorknob as she pulled the door open and stood back for him to leave. When he made no move to, Shea went through the door onto the small veranda and down the few steps.

She crossed her arms, her hands unconsciously rubbing her upper arms, as she turned to face him. 'Well, good-night, Alex. We'll probably see you some time,' she began and Alex gave a soft laugh.

'There's no probably about it, Shea. You will be seeing me.'

Shea sighed. 'All right, Alex. We'll see you,' she repeated flatly and his eyes narrowed in the light from the doorway.

'Niall's a great kid,' he said then and Shea's chin came up, a tightness encircling her heart.

'Thank you,' she murmured a little huskily. 'I think he is.'

'He looks like the Finlays.'

'I suppose he does,' she replied carefully.

'Jamie must have been proud of him.'

'He was.' A cold knot of despair lodged in Shea's throat and threatened to choke her.

'I can't help thinking he could have been mine. My son,' Alex said softly. 'Jamie was a lucky man.'

For the life of her Shea couldn't say a word.

'A son to follow him. And a beautiful wife by his side.' His voice had dropped, the sound drifting across the space between them to run tinglingly over Shea's skin like a low charge of electricity.

Her hands rubbed at her arms again and she shifted from one foot to the other in case he saw her tremble and realised how much his nearness, his words, were affecting her.

'Do you still miss him?'

The unexpectedness of the question made Shea's eyes meet his in surprise. Niall had spoken of the same thing.

'Yes,' she said evenly. How could she not? Jamie had been there when she'd needed him, her steadying refuge, her salvation when Alex had deserted her. 'Yes, I do,' she said more forcefully.

'Yes,' he repeated flatly. 'I miss him, too.'

A cold knot of anger rose inside Shea and she wanted to fly at him, flay him, punish him...

'You hadn't seen him for six years before he died,' she got out through tight lips. 'How can you say you missed him?'

'I missed his letters, his news of Niall. And you.'

Jamie's letters. How could Jamie have kept his contact with Alex from her? Shea thought bitterly. Yet at the same time a voice inside her asked her how Jamie could have told her, knowing how she felt about Alex? Jamie must have been torn between the two of them.

Had Alex written back? He most probably had and she'd never known. Anger rose inside her again, at Jamie as well as Alex.

'I wasn't aware that Jamie wrote to you,' she said, her jaw beginning to ache with her tension.

'He didn't tell you?'

'No. He didn't.'

Alex shrugged. 'Perhaps that's understandable. Maybe he thought you wouldn't want to know.'

Shea's thoughts wavered uncertainly again. In all honesty Jamie would have thought exactly that. And she wouldn't have given Jamie any opportunity to discuss any contact he had with Alex. In the beginning she was so hurt and that hurt had then settled into a blinding anger. Jamie wouldn't have mentioned his cousin for fear of upsetting her.

'I did miss hearing from him though,' Alex added reflectively.

'Oh, I'm sure you did,' Shea retorted scornfully. 'But tell me, Alex. If you missed your cousin so much why didn't you come home for his funeral? There was time for you to get here, if you'd wanted to.'

'Do you think I wouldn't have come if I could have?' he appealed heavily and Shea gave an exclamation of disgust.

'I know, something came up? Another multi-million dollar business deal, I suppose?'

His eyes locked with hers. 'No. It was personal.'

'Oh, I see,' Shea sneered. 'A heavy date, hmmm?'

His hands reached out, fingers digging into her soft flesh as she strained away from him, but he held her fast, his eyes dark pools in his still handsome face, impaling her angrily. They stood like that for long moments until Alex just as suddenly released her and he turned slightly away.

'Nothing like that. But it's a long story and one I don't think you're inclined to hear. Suffice to say I'm deeply sorry I didn't make it home when Jamie died.'

There was a bleakness in his voice that diffused some of Shea's anger and she ran a hand distractedly over her eyes. 'Look, Alex, I'm sorry. I... Perhaps I've got no right to reproach you. I'm just tired I guess. We probably both are. And seeing you brought it all back, Jamie's accident, the media circus, the funeral. You just rubbed me the wrong way.'

'I seem to have been unintentionally doing that all evening,' he said flatly and Shea took a steadying breath.

'I wasn't expecting to see you, that's all,' she replied ineffectually.

'And I wasn't expecting you to be so hostile.'

With no little battle for control Shea refrained from allowing his provocative words to goad her. 'I'm sorry if you feel that way, Alex. But it has been eleven years. You could hardly expect that we'd just—' Shea stopped and swallowed, cursing her wayward tongue.

'That we'd just pick up where we left off?' Alex finished for her. 'Perhaps not. But as I said before, we used to be friends.'

'We were never friends, Alex,' Shea got out bitterly. 'We may have been a lot of things but we were never friends. Not in those last few months anyway.'

'I thought we were. The very best of friends.'

'Friends don't—' Shea pulled herself together. 'I think perhaps you're confusing friendship with sex. We were—'

'We were lovers.' Alex's deep voice snaked down inside her and touched a secret, vulnerably tender nerve.

Words of recrimination, painful condemnation, betrayal, swelled inside her, rose like bile, but she managed to take hold of them before they escaped. 'As I was saying, I think you've misconstrued. We had a physical relationship all those years ago, Alex, one that had nothing to do with anything other than the giving in to salacious lust.'

'I see. A case of sex ruining a beautiful friendship, hmmm?' Alex retorted with no little sarcasm.

'That about covers it, don't you think?' she agreed levelly and Alex gave a harsh laugh.

'Are you serious, Shea?'

She glanced across the space between them. 'Of course.'

Alex shook his head. 'Well, I think it's a joke. And you don't believe it any more than I do. It was never just sex between us.'

He took a step closer to her and Shea gallantly made herself hold her ground. Then he reached out, ran one fingertip softly, incitingly, down the length of her bare arm.

And Shea made no move to escape. The touch of his finger, scarcely more than a shiver on her warm skin, virtually paralysed her good intentions. She knew she couldn't have moved if she'd tried. But she didn't.

'We were one in every sense of the word. Physically. Spiritually. Emotionally.' His voice dropped impossibly, devastatingly, lower. 'Weren't we, Shea?'

Until he left. The words echoed inside Shea and acted like a cascade of cold water on her feverishly hot skin. *Until he left*.

'We were?' She raised her fine eyebrows, dark in one so fair. 'Obviously there's some discrepancy in your recall, Alex.'

'And sarcasm doesn't become you, my dear,' he declared wryly. 'Neither does self-deception.'

'Self-deception?' Shea got out between clenched lips. 'In the beginning, eleven years ago, that term may have been relevant, but not now. Now I can look back without the heightened emotional distortion. We had some fantastic sex, Alex. That was it. And then you left.'

'You know why I went,' he stated flatly.

'You had ambitions and it was easier to follow those ambitions alone, unencumbered.' The words sounded so matter-of-fact. Yet at the time each syllable had been an arrow piercing her aching heart.

'It wasn't as cut and dried as that and you know it, Shea.'

'Wasn't it? I think it was.'

'Then you were wrong. It wasn't. It was the worst, the most difficult decision I've ever had to make in my life. And I thought you understood that.'

Shea shrugged. 'Does it matter now, Alex? It's all water under the bridge.'

'It mattered to me,' he stated succinctly. 'It mattered very much to me, Shea. I asked you to wait a couple of years for me and within the year you'd married someone else, and not just any poor yobbo off the street. You'd married my cousin, Jamie, and you had his child.'

CHAPTER FIVE

'I THINK you'd better go, Alex,' Shea said with all the composure she could muster. 'It's late and I don't think this conversation is going anywhere.'

His steady gaze held hers for long moments before he gave a barely perceptible nod, his fair hair silver in the artificial light. 'You're right, Shea. It is late. But we do need to talk. There are things I want to discuss with you.'

'There's nothing to talk about, Alex. Let's leave the past where it is. I can't see there's anything to be gained by dredging it all up. Now, I...I'll say goodnight.'

He inclined his head again. 'All right. We'll leave it go. For now. Goodnight, Shea.' He turned and climbed into the Jaguar, backing the sleek car out into the street. With a low growl of the car's powerful engine he was gone.

Oblivious, Shea stood looking into the darkness before she realised that in the pool of light from the house she was clearly visible to any of their neighbours who happened to glance her way. She walked quickly up the steps and into the house.

'Are you all right, love?' Norah asked as reluctantly Shea re-entered the kitchen.

'Of course, Norah. I'm fine.' She took a steadying breath and made herself smile. 'Well, that was a surprise, wasn't it?'

'Yes, it was that,' Norah agreed as Shea's eyes briefly held hers before the younger woman turned away and began returning the crockery to the dresser. 'I always expected he'd come back to Byron one day but it was still quite a shock to have him turn up out of the blue.'

'Yes.' Shea kept her concentration on hanging the coffee mugs on their hooks under the high shelf.

'He looks older,' Norah said softly and Shea gave a humourless laugh.

'What did you expect, Norah? That Alex was a modern day Peter Pan? Even Alex Finlay has to grow old. He has no monopoly on youth.'

'I suppose not.' Norah passed Shea the mug she'd been drying. 'But he doesn't look as though life has treated him kindly.'

'Has life been completely kind to any of us?'

Norah sighed. 'You're still bitter about Alex going away, aren't you?'

'Alex made his decision years ago.' Shea shrugged. 'It scarcely matters one way or the other now.'

'I know Alex must have thought what he was doing was for the best,' Norah began and Shea's fingers clutched at the edge of the dresser for support.

The best for Alex Finlay, she thought caustically.

'And he must have been successful in his career,' Norah continued. 'I mean, if he can afford to buy that big white house from the Rostens and then he said he'd bought other property.'

'Did you ever doubt that Alex would be successful?' Shea asked and Norah sighed again.

'No. Not really. He always worked hard and put a hundred percent into everything he did. He deserves any success he's had. But, Shea, seeing him again, well, it's made me realise just how much I missed him all these years.'

Shea swung around to face her mother-in-law. 'Missed him? Norah, he couldn't even come home for Jamie's funeral. How can you of all people forgive him for that?'

'He sent flowers—'

'So did distant acquaintances,' Shea broke in before Norah could make any more excuses for Alex. 'You all but raised him after his own mother died. And so much for his professing to love Jamie like a brother.'

'Oh, Shea, don't be so hard on him. He told me to-night why he didn't come to the funeral.'

'Tonight? Why couldn't he have explained four years ago?'

'He said he wanted to tell me face to face.'

'So what was more important than Jamie's funeral? Did he make another million or so?'

'Patti took an overdose the morning Alex was to fly out,' Norah said softly. 'Alex was at the hospital with her. They didn't think she was going to make it.'

Shea gazed numbly at her mother-in-law and then closed her eyes as a wave of guilt washed over her. She'd just accused Alex of staying away because he was in-volved in a business deal and, even worse, because of a heavy date. How she wished she'd simply kept her sar-castic thoughts to herself and not tried to wound Alex with cheap shots.

Deep down she should have known it would have had to have been something very important to keep Alex away but she'd allowed her bitterness to cast Alex in the worst scenario. But surely she could be excused for wanting to hit out at him?

'I knew in my heart how much Jamie meant to Alex,' Norah was saying, 'that he'd have wanted desperately to be here. But I can understand he wouldn't leave Patti there like that, on her own. He said they'd been sep-arated for some time but she had his phone number in her wallet so the hospital rang him when it happened. Her father was in the UK and someone had to be with her. So Alex stayed.'

'I'm...' Shea wearily expelled a breath and some of the gnawing tension went out of her. 'I'm sorry, Norah. I didn't realise.'

'Alex said she's all right now. You know, I always felt a little sorry for young Patti, back when you all went around together.'

Shea glanced at her mother-in-law in surprise. 'But Patti Rosten had everything anyone could want.' Shea knew Patti had wanted Alex but at the time Shea had thought so trustingly that Alex had loved only her. But Alex had married Patti in the end.

'Oh, Patti had everything in the way of material things,' Norah was saying. 'But she adored her father and he was so busy he rarely had time for her. I saw her as a little lost girl.' Norah shook her head. 'Still, I must say I was surprised when Alex told me he was marrying her.' Norah sighed. 'Alex said she remarried a year or so ago.'

Shea made no comment. Her emotions seemed to have completely switched off and she rubbed a hand across her eyes. 'I'm quite tired, Norah. I think I'll go to bed. I wanted to go into the shop early tomorrow anyway.'

'Yes, we've all had quite a night, haven't we? Goodnight, love. I'll see you in the morning. And Shea.'

She stopped and glanced back at her mother-in-law.

'Alex meant so much to us all.' Norah was obviously choosing her words carefully and Shea tensed. 'I mean, if you feel he needs to make amends or anything, give him the chance to do it.'

'Amends? I doubt Alex thinks he's obliged to explain any of his actions.' Shea gave a strained smile. 'I know I was upset when he left so suddenly but I got over it. As I said before, I don't see that it matters now. My life, our lives, have gone on for eleven years without him. And I can't see our lives changing all that much now that he's back.'

And had she really believed that Norah would take that ridiculous statement on face value? she asked herself as she sat in the darkness of her bedroom a few short hours later. She'd almost laughed at herself as the words left her lips.

Alex's arrival wouldn't change their lives! What a joke on her that had been. Her heartbeats were still racing in the aftermath of her mortifying dream of naked bodies and almost indecent delight.

Shea's skin burned hotly as the theme of her dream came back in all its sensuous clarity. When Alex had first left and she'd realised with panic that he wasn't returning she had had the dream for the first time, the first of many times.

In it she was always with Alex, making love in the moonlight. The settings had sometimes varied but the content and the two participants had been constant.

Late at night when her rigid defences had relaxed, the scene had played through her mind like an R-rated video movie. Each time it was Alex in all his solid masculine beauty that had leapt from her traitorous subconscious to tantalise her. Until she awoke with the excruciatingly electric feel of him so arousingly tangible that it was gut-wrenching agony when she realised it had all been an illusion, and that in reality he would always be lost to her.

Those devastating dreams had continued even after she'd married Jamie. At least while their marriage had remained as platonic as their previous relationship.

Dear Jamie. He'd married her knowing she was carrying his cousin's child and that she couldn't bear him or any other man to touch her. He'd stayed with her throughout Niall's difficult birth. And he'd loved Niall as he would have loved his own son.

Strangely, hearing Alex was engaged to marry Patti Rosten had somehow changed Shea's whole life. It was as though her frozen heart had begun to thaw. It had been painful but she'd survived. And she'd once again turned to Jamie for comfort and solace. Their marriage may not have set anything on fire but they cared deeply for each other. And they both loved Niall.

Shea drew up her knees and dropped her weary head onto them. If only she could have taken the love she'd lavished on Alex, the love he'd thrust so callously back at her, and given it to Jamie. Jamie had earned it, and more. He'd saved her sanity when Alex left. Certainly Jamie had deserved more than what she'd had to offer him.

Looking back, Shea could scarcely credit she had been as carefree, as secure, in Alex's love as she had been all those years ago. And that particular night, the night he'd broken her young heart, was burned into her memory, each scene seemingly etched indelibly with painful precision.

Alex had taken her out to dinner, to their favourite restaurant. They'd eaten spaghetti and finished off the meal with fresh fruit and homemade ice cream.

Shea had noticed Alex had been a little quiet all evening but she'd been so euphoric about what she had to tell him that she'd seemed to float through the meal in some sort of pleasurable daze. She hadn't even considered that Alex may not be as ecstatic as she was about their baby.

After the meal they drove to their favourite spot and Alex suggested they go for a walk along the deserted beach. More than pleasantly full after the meal, Shea had happily agreed. They kicked off their shoes and Shea slipped her hand into Alex's as she always did.

They walked some distance and then started back and as they neared the spot where Alex had left his car the moon had slid from behind some thin cottonwool-like clouds and lit the beach.

'Mmmm,' Shea murmured appreciatively. 'Isn't this the most beautiful place on earth, Alex?' She snuggled closer to his hard body and the heady mixture of the scent of sand and sea and the faint musky aroma of his aftershave teased her nostrils, made her yearn for him to take her in his strong arms the way he always did.

Then she'd tell him about the baby. She could see the scene. She'd shyly disclose the momentous news and he'd clasp her to him, holding her gently, as though she were a fragile flower. He'd kiss her reverently and then she'd laughingly tell him that she wouldn't break, that it was all a very natural part of life, that the doctor had pronounced her fit and healthy, and that having a baby didn't mean an end to making love.

And then that's just what they'd do. Make love. And make plans to be together forever.

Alex stopped walking and Shea stood on tiptoe, her lips nibbling his earlobe. But instead of turning to her Alex had stepped away.

'Shea, we have to talk.'

'I know.' She frowned slightly. Could Alex already know she was pregnant? Of course he couldn't. They thought they'd been so careful, Alex always using a contraceptive. Apart from that first time. Shea smiled to herself. But that one and only time had been enough to make their child.

'Shea, I—' Alex stopped and ran his hand unsteadily through his hair. 'You know I want to further my education, that I planned to keep my job at the surf shop and go to Uni part-time?'

Shea nodded.

'Well, that would take years longer than full-time study.'

'But I thought you couldn't afford to go to Uni full-time, even with the partial scholarship you got,' Shea began.

'I couldn't. That's why this idea of Joe Rosten's is so great. He wants to pay me to do my course and then go to work for him. He'll pay all my tuition, living expenses, etc. It's a dream come true.'

'You mean, Mr Rosten's sort of giving you a full-time scholarship?'

'Something like that. Of course, I'd have to go to work for him after I get my degree but that's no problem. There's hundreds of people who'd kill for this. I get my qualifications and I have a job waiting for me at the end of it.' Alex shook his head. 'Part of me still can't believe it.'

'Alex, it sounds wonderful. When did he ask you? And how come he asked you?'

'He came into the shop yesterday with Patti and we started talking about my plans and suddenly he simply made me this offer. Then, last night, he came over and talked to Dad and I about it. You know Dad and Joe go way back. They met when Joe was stationed out here during the war?'

'Oh, Alex. I can't believe it, either.' Shea hugged him. 'Which university will you be going to? I guess Queensland would be closer.'

'Well, that's just it, Shea. Joe's going back to the States and he wants me to go with him, attend his old alma mater.'

'You mean he wants you to go live in the States?' Shea asked incredulously and Alex nodded. 'But that's such a big upheaval. What does your father think about it?'

Alex shrugged. 'Dad doesn't mind. It's not as though Joe's a stranger. Dad's kept in touch with him since the war and Joe wants Dad to come over for a visit, too. You know Joe and Patti were only staying in Byron for the summer anyway.'

Shea felt her mouth tighten. And all summer Patti Rosten had been throwing herself at Alex. Not that he'd noticed, but— Shea felt the first tremor of disquiet. 'But Mr Rosten bought the big white house,' she said hopefully.

'Just for investment. Joe and Patti are going back next week and they want me to go with them.'

Did Alex mean he was going without her? A feeling of light-headedness almost overcame her but she managed to regain control.

'Why go so soon?' she got out. Maybe she would follow him later?

'It seems sensible. I can get settled. Joe's letting me have a small flat attached to his place and I can do some pre-course study.'

A curlew gave a distant eerie cry that echoed in the moonlight and Shea suddenly felt cold. Alex had made no mention of her.

'What about me?' The words slipped thinly through her tense lips and fell between them, turned the moist air around them into a heavy swirling tension.

'You know how I feel about you, Shea,' Alex said carefully. 'But I've been thinking about us and, well, I feel so bloody guilty because you're so young and I shouldn't have taken advantage of that.'

'Taken advantage? You mean we shouldn't have made love?'

'No, we shouldn't have. You're so young and—'

'Alex, for heaven's sake. I'm hardly a child and I was way over the age of consent.'

Alex raised his hands and let them fall. 'I meant that you were inexperienced and—'

'I knew enough to know I love you, Alex. I always have.'

'And I love you, too. But the time's not right, Shea. You need to, well, see a bit more of life.'

'Try another man?' Shea cried angrily, her fear clutching deep inside her.

'God, no! I didn't mean that. I just—' Alex shook his head. 'I mean you're only seventeen, too young to settle down.'

'Why can't I come with you? I could get a job, too.'

'I just think I need to do this on my own for a while. I need to give this a concentrated effort, no distractions.'

'I'd be a distraction? Is that how you see me?'

'You know that's not what I meant. At the moment I have nothing to offer you, Shea. Except poverty. I don't even own that clapped-out old car. I want more for you.'

'I just want you, Alex,' Shea said brokenly.

'That's not enough as I see it.' Alex's voice sounded unnaturally thick but Shea could only see her own pain.

'Look, Shea. It will only be for a few years. I'll get my degree—'

'A few years? Alex, please. I don't want to be apart from you for a day, let alone a few years. I need you now.'

Alex turned away, his broad shoulders hunched. And then he straightened and turned back to face her. 'Shea, I'm flattered you think you feel that way and if you still do in a couple of years, well, then we can make plans.'

'Make plans? I thought we already had made plans, Alex.'

'We're just postponing them for a while. Shea, please. Don't make this any harder for me.'

'Any harder for you!' Shea's voice rose. 'My God, Alex! You're an arrogant, despicable bastard and I hate you. I hate you!'

He moved towards her but she took a step away from him.

'No! Don't touch me! I do really hate you, Alex. And I never want to see you again.' He reached for her again, tried to take hold of her but she thrust him from her and, stepping awkwardly in an indentation, he fell backward, measuring his length in the soft sand.

Shea turned and sprinted across the beach, crawled up the grassy dune and was across the verge to the road by the time Alex appeared over the bank. As luck would have it a taxi passed at that moment and frantically Shea hailed it, falling into the back as Alex raced across to the road. She watched him standing impotently in the moonlight as the taxi pulled away.

For five days she refused to see him and wouldn't take his calls. Eventually, when Alex was due to leave the following day, it was Jamie who convinced her to speak to him.

'Do you still think we should wait for years, Alex?' she'd asked him flatly.

'Shea, I don't want us to part like this—' Alex began.

'Do you still want to go to the States on your own?' Shea repeated, and there was a heavy silence.

'Yes, Shea. I do. You're young and—'

'Then there's really no more to be said, is there?' Shea cut in on him. 'Goodbye, Alex. Have a wonderful time.'

Shea sighed brokenly and lay back against her pillows. In retrospect, from the safety of eleven years on, she could acknowledge that part of her pain had been self-inflicted. She could recognise now that nothing anyone could have said back then would have changed her focus, for she had been totally consumed by her love for Alex.

With the self-centred arrogance and naïvety of youth she had simply adored him, had built him into some kind of god. Then when she'd discovered her god had feet of clay, that he'd fallen from the pedestal she'd blindly placed him on, she had very nearly crumpled right along with him.

If she were honest she'd admit that no one could have lived up to her fanciful ideals. Certainly not an ambitious, attractive twenty-one-year-old who was handed a future he'd only dreamed about.

Shea plumped her pillows restlessly and closed her eyes, willing the oblivion of sleep. Alex had only been back in her life for mere hours and here she was making excuses for him.

And Alex's face kept slipping so easily into her mind, as though she'd held that particular place void, waiting for him to return. Irritably she made herself examine the picture of him.

He was definitely older, any remaining boyish softness gone from the now craggy lines of his features. But he was just as devastatingly attractive.

Shea groaned softly as she fought to repudiate that thought. How could she deny a fact that was so obviously true? Alex Finlay still possessed that fascinatingly elusive quality that made everyone take a second look. And the maturity he now wore like a badge made him even more appealing... To anyone who was not resistant to his attractions, Shea reminded herself forcefully. And if anyone should have that specific immunity, she should have.

But did she? The question rose to taunt her. Part of her recognised just how easy it would be to fall under his spell again. She'd thought she'd lost everything last time but now she had so much more to lose.

Niall. Her heart contracted painfully. If Alex found out he had a son would he try to take Niall from her? No. Alex wouldn't do that. Would he?

How would she know after all this time? Eleven years ago she would have said not, but she didn't have such a good track record when it came to understanding Alex Finlay.

Even if he wanted to have some input in Niall's life, could she in all fairness deny him that? Shea steeled herself. She could and would. Biology was only a small part of being a parent. In every other aspect Jamie had been Niall's father and Alex had no rights.

Shea sat up again, wide awake now. No rights? Had she given Alex the chance to have any rights? But by his actions he had forfeited those rights.

She continued to agonise over it all, fighting to include the politics of her predicament in a situation she knew she was only seeing emotionally.

For what remained of the night Shea tossed and turned agitatedly and it was with more than a little relief that she switched off her clock radio alarm and climbed from her dishevelled bed. With a shiver she decided that the state of her bedclothes gave every indication that her erotic dream could well have been reality.

Well, it wasn't! she told herself angrily and, collecting her clothes, she headed for the bathroom. She stood under the shower for longer than usual, letting the tepid water course over her, and only climbed out when the thought slid into her mind that perhaps she might be trying to wash away her night's graphic illusory dalliances.

Towelling herself dry with great vigour she dressed in a light coral pink straight skirt and matching short-sleeved tailored jacket. She gazed at her reflection in the mirror and determinedly pulled herself together.

Make-up would disguise the dark shadows beneath her eyes but she'd have to mentally suppress these continuous and unnecessary nostalgic thoughts of Alex. The shock of his return had obviously unleashed this monster she'd been harbouring within herself but now that the surprise of his reappearance had worn off she should be able to put it all back into perspective, leave the past and get on again with the present.

Of course, she reflected later as she entered her office, it hadn't helped that Niall had arrived at the breakfast table none the worse for his interrupted night's sleep, bright-eyed and singing Alex's praises. Every second sentence seemed to begin with Alex and Shea was more than a little relieved to leave her son to finish his breakfast with his grandmother.

Sue Gavin, her next door neighbour, was going to deliver her son, Pete, and Niall to school this morning so Shea could take the opportunity to get to work early and catch up on some of her office work. Her paperwork seemed to have multiplied threefold as she prepared to expand her business into larger premises.

With resolution she put Alex out of her mind and, by the time Debbie, her young assistant, arrived, Shea could congratulate herself on making a reasonable amount of headway.

'Lovely day, Shea.' Debbie breezed in like a breath of fresh air and set a steaming mug of coffee on the desk in front of Shea.

She took a sip and murmured her grateful thanks. 'Mmmm. That's wonderful. Remind me to give you a raise,' she said lightly and Debbie laughed.

'You only say that when there are no witnesses.'

'No. I'm serious, Debbie. As of this week. I really appreciate what a great job you do and the fact that I can safely leave you here when I'm out of the shop.'

Debbie flushed with pleasure. 'Well, thanks, Shea.'

'And now that we've expanded our floor space I think we definitely need to get you an assistant. The shop's too big for one person to handle, especially as it takes me longer to visit our outlets these days.' Shea took another gulp of coffee. 'So if you know of anyone you think would be suitable, please tell them to give me a call.'

'That would be great.' Debbie shifted from one foot to the other. 'Um. As a matter of fact I do know someone. My young cousin, Megan.'

Shea frowned. 'Which one is she?'

'Uncle Mick's daughter. Remember my aunt died a couple of years ago? Megan's been sort of looking after the family. She has three younger brothers. But her father's just remarried, someone they all like, luckily, and now Megan wants to get a job. She's a nice kid, just turned eighteen, and very responsible and reliable.'

'Perhaps you could ask her when she could come in for an interview.'

'I could ring her now. I'm sure she'd be free,' Debbie said eagerly and Shea laughed.

'Okay. Tell her to come in about four o'clock this afternoon.'

'Great.' Debbie beamed and went to hurry off. 'Oh, I heard some rabble-rousers at the meeting last night wanted to stage a sit-in at the council chambers. I can just see David Aston leading the parade with his placard.'

Shea laughed despite herself. 'I think the picketing idea was all talk.'

'Pity. It would liven the place up. And talking about that, I also heard a guy who used to live in Byron turned up. Alex Finlay. Isn't he a relative of yours?'

'Jamie's cousin,' Shea said evenly, her gaze going from Debbie's interested face to the pile of papers on her desk.

'And isn't he the guy whose photograph's on the wall at the high school?'

Shea raised her eyebrows. 'It's at least fifteen years since Alex went to that school.'

'He's something of a legend there. He used to be the school captain, didn't he?'

'Oh, yes.' Shea nodded casually. 'I think he was.'

'I thought so,' Debbie continued enthusiastically. 'Footballer. Surfer. Dux of the school. Wow! He's just gorgeous. What a spunk. All those blond curls and come-to-bed eyes. I could really go for him.'

Shea almost cringed but made a great show of shuffling her papers. 'That photo was taken years ago,' she reminded the younger woman. 'I'm afraid the blond curls have gone,' she added, thrusting aside the very vivid memories of her fingers tangling in those same blond curls.

'Maybe I could talk him into growing them again.' Debbie grinned cheekily. 'Unless he's bald. That would be a catastrophe.'

'No, he's not bald,' Shea said before she could prevent herself.

'What a relief.' Debbie wiped her brow theatrically. 'I'm not usually into older men but if Alex Finlay is anything like his photograph I could make an exception.'

Shea glanced at her wristwatch. 'I think it's almost time to open the shop,' she said a little sharply and then felt mean as Debbie's bright expression faded. She made herself smile. 'We don't want to keep the hoards of early customers waiting, do we?'

Debbie's easy smile returned. 'No way. Oh.' She turned back again and Shea steeled herself for more extravagant exclamations of Alex's attributes. 'And don't forget the dashing David Aston's coming at nine o'clock this morning to take you out on a factory crawl.'

Shea glanced at the time again. 'Oh, yes. That's right. I had forgotten.' All this brouhaha about Alex had put her appointment with David completely out of her mind. 'I'm determined to make a final decision on the new building today. I'm sick of having that particular decision hanging over my head. And, apart from that, spending my time looking at the pros and cons of empty old industrial sheds doesn't exactly turn me on.'

'Not even when you go looking with David Aston?'

Shea raised her eyebrows at Debbie. 'David? No, not even with him.'

Debbie grinned. 'I'll bet he wouldn't say the same. He's like a sad-eyed puppy around you, Shea.'

'That's ridiculous, Debbie.'

'If you say so.' Debbie chuckled and went to open the door of the shop.

Shea frowned reflectively. Not only had she forgotten her appointment with David Aston but she hadn't even given the young man a thought since Alex had rudely dismissed him the evening before.

Debbie was right. David had made a few tentative overtures towards her, Shea knew that, but she had refused to even consider giving him any encouragement, neatly deflecting his hesitant advances. She wasn't interested in starting a relationship with anyone, let alone an intense young man like David. He was a nice enough person but he was, she admitted somewhat contritely, and as Niall had intimated, just a little boring.

Shea hadn't worried unduly about his more than professional interest in her because she hoped her persistent indifference would discourage him. And once she found the right factory space for her proposed expansions she would have no need to continue any dealings with him. She knew she could have asked for a different representative from the real estate agency but that may have reflected badly on David and his career. She'd decided a firm distancing of herself would do the trick and thus far it had.

David Aston walked into *Shea Finlay* at precisely nine o'clock, as Shea knew he would. He was always punctual, always immaculately dressed, as he was today. His neatly pressed pale green shirt toned in with his darker brown-green slacks, both complemented by his multi-autumn-coloured tie. He gave off a pleasant unobtrusive odour of spicy aftershave as he approached Shea with a broad smile.

'Wonderful news, Shea. We've managed to track down a representative of the company that owns the collection of factories out along the road into town.'

'The building I've preferred all along? David, that's great. Can we go out there first?' Shea couldn't suppress her excitement.

The building David was referring to was one she'd seen herself before she'd consulted the real estate agency, but until now no one had been able to contact the owners of the half dozen large, newly built business premises. As far as industrial buildings went, the six new buildings were modernly styled and pleasing to the eye. Not the standard bland and ugly rectangular boxes usually associated with industry.

David slipped back the cuff of his shirt and frowned down at his wristwatch. 'Charlie left me a message that the representative couldn't meet us out there until after ten, so we may as well refresh our memories with the other premises you've shown an interest in.'

Shea sighed softly as she collected her shoulder bag. It seemed as though David wasn't going to be hurried over this so she may as well resign herself to the fact and go with the flow. But if the building she'd seen a month or so ago was available for lease it would be ideal.

Shea tried to quell a spurt of anticipation. She mustn't allow herself to get too excited in case she was disappointed. Perhaps the owner would already have occupants for the buildings or maybe the rental prices would be too high.

David opened the door of his car with a flourish and Shea slid inside with a faint feeling of déjà vu. Less than twenty-four hours ago she'd done the same thing, with no inkling of what the evening was to hold.

As David walked around the front of the car she found herself appraising him again. His dark hair was cut in a conservative short back and sides style and he must keep a battery-driven razor in his car for she'd never seen him show the slightest sign of the 'five o'clock shadow' of most dark-haired men. He was quite nice-looking, tall with an average build.

But David couldn't hold a candle to Alex Finlay. Shea straightened in the seat. Where had that thought come from? She hadn't even been thinking about Alex. And comparing David to him was unfair to the younger man.

'I'm glad you got home safely after the meeting.' David was clipping his seatbelt into place beside her and Shea shifted disconcertedly.

'Yes, I did. Thank you for ringing to check but it wasn't necessary, David. I mean, there was no need for you to worry. I've,' Shea swallowed tensely, 'known Alex since I was a child.'

'You didn't expect him back?'

'No. We haven't really kept in touch,' she said indifferently, hoping David would get the message and change the subject. Alex Finlay had been everyone's topic of conversation this morning, Shea frowned irritatedly, beginning with Niall at breakfast, then Debbie and now David Aston. And quite frankly, Shea was tired of it.

Oblivious of Shea's thoughts David started the car and pulled out from the curb. 'He struck me as being a guy who likes his own way. Not something that goes down too well with you women these days, wouldn't you agree?'

Shea murmured non-committally and she felt David slide a sideways glance at her.

'Will you be going to the markets this weekend?' he asked, setting the conversation onto safer ground, and Shea relaxed a little.

'Of course.' Shea always went to Byron Bay's monthly market days. It was at the markets that she'd really got her start, beginning to sell the clothes she'd designed and made, and her business had expanded from there. She still had her own stall and she took turns with Debbie to run it. As David knew. So perhaps the ground wasn't quite as safe as she'd imagined it was a moment ago.

'I hear they're having a beach concert after the markets this month,' David continued a trifle reticently. 'I just wondered if you'd considered going?'

Was David asking her to go with him? Shea felt herself
flush a little. Well, she had no intention of doing so and
her first impulse was to bluntly tell him so. But she didn't
want to offend him. 'Niall mentioned something about
it but I'm not sure if we will. So, where will we be heading
first this morning?' she hurried on, forcing a brightness
into her voice she was far from feeling.

For the next hour they visited three other prospective
sites for Shea's business expansions and then they headed
out along the road which led from the Pacific Highway
into Byron Bay. The new estate was a couple of miles
from the centre of town.

David pulled up in front of a small mobile office which
hadn't been in evidence the last time they'd looked at
the outside of the buildings. No one was around so they
walked across to the first building, Shea standing on
tiptoe to peer in through the glass window.

'This one's the exact size I had in mind. In fact it
would be perfect. They all seem to have their own parking
areas and there'd be no congestion around the loading
bays. And the fact that the buildings are far enough apart
and are so wonderfully landscaped to be relatively se-
cluded as far as noise, etc., goes is a big plus. Don't you
think so, David?'

'Oh, I agree, Shea.' David nodded seriously.

'And Charlie didn't say who owned them?'

'No. He just left me the message that he'd made the
appointment. He got away early this morning to do some
property valuations down the coast.'

Shea frowned. 'The only drawback I can see is the
fact that, as the buildings are new they may be too expensive for me.'

'I'm sure the owner will be open to negotiation,' David
said confidently. 'Times are hard and people aren't as
keen to start small businesses as they were a few years

ago. And it's always good to get tenants into one building to encourage others to follow.'

'I hope you're right,' Shea began, only to break off as they heard a car turn into the service road and stop behind the makeshift office.

David and Shea walked quickly back the way they'd come and as they rounded the end of the office Shea's steps faltered and then stopped. She stifled a gasp of surprise as she gazed in amazement at the man climbing from the dark sports car.

CHAPTER SIX

THAT Alex was as taken aback as she was Shea recognised in the slight raising of his eyebrows but he merely nodded to them before turning to fit a key into the office door. He then stood back for them to precede him up the two steps and into the room.

'Well, what a surprise!' David also seemed to have recovered from his astonishment and put on his most professional bonhomie. 'I didn't expect last night that we'd be seeing each other again so soon. David Aston,' David reminded him brightly and held out his hand. 'And Alex Finlay, wasn't it?'

Alex silently inclined his fair head and, setting his leather briefcase on the desk, he took David's outstretched hand.

'Charlie Gray said we would meet a rep from the company handling the leasing of these buildings. I take it that's you?' David smiled earnestly and with obvious reluctance, Alex acknowledged his question. 'Good. Good.' David put a proprietary hand on Shea's arm. 'And, of course, Alex, you already know Shea.'

Alex turned his brown eyes on Shea. 'Yes, I do.' His deep voice ran shivers along her nerve endings and she felt her entire body begin to ache with tension.

'I suppose Charlie will also have told you we may have one or two people interested in these buildings.' David rubbed his hands together. 'Ideal situation this but a great pity the economic climate isn't a trifle healthier.'

Alex's brown gaze had remained on Shea and she felt the beginnings of a flush warm her neck.

'Won't you sit down,' he said at last and motioned to the two chairs behind them.

David made a show of holding one chair for Shea to be seated and Alex strode around the desk and sat down himself.

'So, what interest do you have in the buildings, Shea?' Alex asked levelly, pointedly ignoring David.

'Shea's thinking of expanding the manufacturing side of her business,' David began.

'What sort of floor space are we talking about?' Alex relaxed back in his seat and motioned David to silence when the other man would have again answered on Shea's behalf.

Just at that moment Shea's vocal chords seemed disinclined to function so she was glad David was there to reply to Alex's questions and she seethed at his blatant rudeness towards the younger man. What did Alex expect anyway? David was, after all, representing her, so he would assume Alex would want to deal with him.

How Shea wished she could simply stand and walk away. But somehow or other Alex was part of the company involved with the new buildings and it seemed she was going to have to deal with him over the lease if she wanted it. And she did.

Well, she was a businesswoman, she reminded herself, and this was purely a business deal. Pulling herself together, Shea cleared her throat and proceeded to outline her factory needs.

Alex listened attentively and he remained silent when she was finished.

'Of course, Shea will want to have a closer look at the building before she makes a decision,' David put in quickly. 'And she'll be looking for the best deal as far as the lease goes.'

'I can supply business references, should you need them,' Shea added.

'Her company's sound and she has exemplary credentials,' David cut in and Alex regarded him levelly, making David shift nervously in his seat.

'I'm sure she has,' Alex remarked drily and reached into his briefcase and extracted a bunch of keys. 'Which building or buildings are you interested in?'

'This first one here.' David pointed out the building that was visible from the office and Alex passed him the key.

'I have some paperwork to do so please take your time.' With that Alex drew out a folder and opened it in front of him, indicating their discussions were at an end for the moment.

David and Shea crossed the verge from the office to the building and David unlocked the door.

'Was he always so belligerent? Or is it just me?' David asked peevishly as they stepped inside.

'I can't recall,' Shea muttered vaguely and dug in her bag for her tape.

David helped her take some measurements and she jotted them down in her notebook. Her excitement built and for a moment she almost forgot that Alex had anything to do with this deal, that he was sitting in his office nearby.

'Shall I go back and sound him out about his prices while you finish looking over the building?' David asked and Shea shook her head.

'I shouldn't be too long and we can go together.'

'I just think it would be better if you let me discuss it with him. You shouldn't have to do this wheeling and dealing. That's what I'm paid to do. I'm your agent and I should earn my money.' David gave her a weak smile.

'All right.' She agreed reluctantly and watched David stride off purposefully.

She sighed. If David thought he could outmanoeuvre someone of Alex's calibre he was in for a shock. But business was business and Alex surely wouldn't ask an outlandish rental just because it was Shea who wanted to lease the building. Would he? If the answer was in the affirmative there was precious little she could say to change it.

Shea finished her inspection and walked across to the open door. Reluctant to rejoin Alex and David, she gave a sigh of relief when David came around the corner of the office alone and hurried across to her.

'Finished?' he asked with a frown and Shea's heart sank.

'What did he say?' she appealed and David took her arm.

'Not here.' He looked meaningfully towards the office. 'Come on. We can talk in the car.'

As they walked across the asphalt Shea felt the burning stab of Alex's eyes on them and she was thankful when David had turned the car out onto the highway and they were heading back towards town.

'I think we could both use a cup of coffee, don't you?' David said with feeling and Shea sat silently gazing at the area she knew so well, her eyes not really registering it.

What she really wanted was to go back to work, immerse herself in the repetitive familiarity of her invoices and orders. But she knew she'd have to hear what David had to tell her and she also knew from past experience that David took his job seriously and wouldn't be rushed. He always insisted they leave any discussions until they were seated back at his office and the receptionist had provided coffee.

However, he didn't turn right at the roundabout as she'd expected he would, but drove straight ahead.

Shea shifted in her seat. 'I thought we were going back to the office.'

David gave her a crooked smile. 'It's such a nice sunny day I thought the Beach Café might be better than the office. OK?'

Shea nodded reluctantly and sat silently until he'd parked the car under a tree near the well-known eatery.

They were a little early for the lunch-time influx of customers and David chose a table out on the deck, seeing Shea seated before going to place their order. The other half dozen or so patrons, obviously tourists, were exclaiming over the panoramic view of the Pacific Ocean.

Shea followed their admiring gazes and felt some of the tension leave her, to be replaced by a sense of fatalism. Alex was apparently going to be perverse. So be it. She sighed. Looking at the beauty of this view, who couldn't help but put aside some of life's small obstacles, she thought wryly. She had all but decided she wouldn't be able to have that particular building weeks ago. Nothing had really changed.

She let her eyes drink in the scene, the incredible blue of the sky and the turquoise deepening to indigo ocean that seemed to stretch to infinity. And off to the right from the heights of the lighthouse on the point, Australia's most easterly point, she knew the view was even more spectacular. It seemed from up there that you really could see forever.

David returned and sat down opposite her, following her gaze out over the water as she reluctantly brought her thoughts back to the business of the building lease.

'Who could even think of polluting the oceans when you look at those magnificent colours?' David remarked. 'The wonderful views were what made me settle here.'

Shea shifted a little irritatedly in her seat. 'So what did Alex say?' she repeated, unable to curb her curiosity a moment longer. But to her exasperation the young waitress chose that moment to set down a tray containing two steaming cups of coffee and David waited until the girl had left them.

'He's the most bloody-minded—' David stopped and looked apologetically at her. 'I'm sorry, Shea. Please excuse my rudeness. But Alex Finlay really is the limit.'

So Alex *was* going to make her life difficult again. Why had she expected that it would be any different? From the moment she saw him last night she'd known the even pace of her life was about to change. And she'd known it wouldn't be for the better.

See! she wanted to scream at that small vulnerable part of her that had soared excitedly at his reappearance. See! Alex Finlay hasn't changed at all.

'You mean he won't consider my application for the lease?' she asked flatly and David set his coffee cup back down and leaned towards her.

'He didn't say that exactly.'

Shea raised her eyebrows. 'What did he say then?'

'Not much.' David sat back and frowned. 'Just that he'd think it over.'

'Think it over? Think what over? The terms of the lease? Or having my business in his building?' Shea added before she could draw the comment back, but David didn't seem surprised by her implication.

'I have no idea, Shea. Oh, he took a copy of the usual leasing contract and said he'd look it over and get back to me. But he simply wouldn't discuss business with me. It's highly irregular.'

Shea took a sip of her coffee. What was Alex playing at?

'Maybe he's just being cautious about the contract. I mean, I told him it was a standard contract, that we were a firm built on integrity. I assured him there were no problems with the economic state of your business and that you were interested in a long-term lease. You'd have thought he'd have jumped at the offer.'

David continued in this vein while Shea tried to account for Alex's reluctance to do business with her. Was he going to deny her the factory space simply because of, well, because of their past? Surely not. Alex was an astute businessman. He wouldn't—

'I have a gut feeling he'll come around.' David interrupted her thoughts. 'Perhaps he likes to play his hand this way. Keep us guessing. But I wouldn't worry too much about it, Shea,' he added reassuringly.

'I can always choose one of the other buildings,' Shea said ruefully. 'That building did seem a little too good to be true. And it would be just my luck to get a heavy engineering shop next door anyway.'

'No worries there. Finlay said he definitely didn't want anything like that. Thinks it's too close to town. The guy's very environment-conscious it would seem, even if he is a trifle unusual in the way he does business,' he added scornfully.

'I'll go and see him about it myself,' Shea said and David pursed his lips.

'I don't think that's necessary. I'm your representative. That's what you pay me for.' He gave a crooked smile. 'I think the best thing might be to wait him out.'

And Shea was still churning over Alex's apparent perversity when she turned into her driveway after work. She didn't want to wait anyone out. She wanted to get on with her business expansion and she'd do just that. With or without Alex's building.

Shea noticed Niall's bicycle was in the car port and she walked up the steps, expecting him to greet her. But he wasn't in his room and she walked on towards the kitchen.

'Hi, Norah!' she greeted her mother-in-law who was busy preparing the evening meal.

Norah gave Shea a wan smile as Shea sat down opposite her.

'Aren't you feeling well?' Shea asked with concern.

'Oh, I'm all right, love. Just my pesky gall bladder playing up as usual.' Norah grimaced. 'That's what I get for having some cream-filled sponge for morning tea over at Sue's next door.'

'Here, let me help you with that.' Shea began dicing the vegetables. 'Did you call the doctor?'

'It wasn't that bad, love. I took some of my medicine and I'm almost back to normal. Don't worry,' Norah added when Shea went to remonstrate her. 'I'd call Doctor Robbins if I thought it was necessary.'

'OK. You just make sure you do. And no more cream cake for a while.' Shea patted the older woman's hand.

'No more cream cake period,' Norah agreed with feeling. 'Nothing worse than an ailment that's self-inflicted.'

Shea smiled. 'Where's Niall by the way? Over at Pete's? I saw his bike in the garage and thought he'd be here.'

'Oh, Pete's bicycle is out of action with a broken chain so they went off for a walk instead of a ride.'

Shea glanced at the clock. 'It's getting late. Did they say where they were going?'

'I told them to be home before six.' Norah was busying herself checking the roast chicken in the oven. 'They went down towards the beach to see Alex. Remember? Alex told Niall last night he could go down and have a look at the house.'

Shea had stopped dicing the carrots. 'He went down to see Alex?' The same constricting pain clutched at Shea's heart.

'Alex did ask him,' Norah began.

'But Niall didn't have to go today. Alex has only just arrived and, well—' Shea swallowed as her mother-in-law straightened from the oven. 'I was going to, I mean,

I intended taking him down myself one day,' she finished lamely.

'He'll be all right with Alex, love,' Norah said softly and Shea stood up and paced the kitchen.

She came to a decision. 'Look, Norah, I'd prefer it if Niall didn't get too involved with Alex.'

Norah wiped her hands on her apron and met Shea's gaze.

'I don't think it's a good idea,' Shea continued in a rush. 'Alex has just arrived home and we haven't seen him for years. How do we know what he's like now?'

'Alex was always very responsible,' Norah began and Shea agitatedly pushed a strand of hair that had escaped from her chignon back behind her ear.

'That's not exactly what's worrying me. I don't want Niall getting too close to him. Alex is just as likely to up and leave as quickly as he arrived. And where will that leave Niall?'

'Niall's not a baby, love. He'd understand if that happened. I think you're making too much of it. At the moment Alex is a novelty. Things will settle into their rightful place in time.'

Shea turned away. Their rightful place? What if she told Norah—

'You know how much Niall misses Jamie, Norah, and because there's a slight family resemblance he might, you know...' Shea left the end of her sentence hanging, afraid to actually say the words out loud.

'Substitute Alex as a father figure,' Norah finished quietly for her and Shea sat back down at the table, her legs suddenly weak.

But the knot of anger inside her still burned. 'I can't accept Alex as part of some happy families charade,' she got out. 'I was too angry when he left and it took me too long to deal with that anger. I don't want to dredge it up again.'

'I can understand that, love, but believe me, life's too short to keep a hold of unhappiness. It can eat away at you, even make you ill.' Norah sighed. 'Can't you just put all that behind you and maybe get to know Alex again? You were such good friends once. I think he'd like to be that again.'

'Friends?' Shea almost laughed. 'Alex said much the same actually. But I just can't.' She shook her head. 'I mean, what did he expect? That I'd welcome him back here with open arms? You don't understand how—' Shea stopped and bit her lip.

She'd come so close then to confiding in Norah the secret she'd only shared with Jamie. But as Jamie's mother, Norah was the last person she could tell. She loved Norah as much as she would have loved her own mother if she were alive and to unburden herself to Norah, tell her that her beloved grandson was not her grandson, would surely break the older woman's heart. And she couldn't bring herself to do that. Not after all Norah had done for her, for them all.

'You loved Alex very much, didn't you?' Norah asked softly and Shea ran a tired hand over her eyes.

'Yes, I did. But not anymore.'

'You never talked about that time. About Alex,' Norah prompted and Shea again felt the almost overwhelming need to confess, to let the whole sordid sequence of events see the light of day. But she didn't.

Instead, she pushed herself to her feet again. 'As you said, Norah, it was all a long time ago. Let's just leave it that I feel Alex and I have grown too far apart the past eleven years. There's a gap that's difficult to bridge, even if either of us wanted to.' She glanced at the time again. 'It's ten to six. I think I'll get the car out and go down and pick the boys up. They're probably on their way home by now.'

Norah looked as if she was about to say something but changed her mind. 'All right. It is a bit of a walk for them.'

Shea climbed into the car and backed out onto the road. No matter what Norah said about Alex being someone different in Niall's life she was going to have to have a talk with her son. She didn't want him plaguing Alex all the time.

And she didn't want Alex and Niall getting too close. The thought slipped into her mind and she tried to examine it dispassionately. But, of course, she couldn't. When it came to the subject of Alex Finlay she was emotional enough. But when she added her son to the equation her turmoil only trebled.

She drove down along the shortest route the boys would take but saw no sign of them. With no little reluctance, she turned off the road and drove between the huge open wrought-iron gates of the big white house that used to be owned by the wealthy American, Joe Rosten, but now apparently belonged to Alex.

As Niall had said, the painters had been at work and the house was now a rich cream with rusty brown trim, giving it a distinctively Spanish flavour. She followed the curve of the drive and pulled up before she reached the impressive front entrance. Alex's dark maroon Jaguar was visible through the open door of the huge garage.

Forcing herself to get out of the car she suddenly remembered she'd suggested to David that she consult Alex herself about the lease and she almost laughed. She had no wish to see Alex again about anything but as Niall was presumably here it seemed she would have to. Taking a steadying breath she made herself walk up the few steps and rang the bell.

Alex opened the door himself. He'd changed from the dark suit he'd worn earlier in the day and was now casually dressed in faded jeans and an old light sweatshirt.

The sweatshirt was light blue and had short sleeves and a hood which lay back from Alex's shoulders, the ties dangling over his broad chest. And Shea remembered that sweatshirt so well it brought a painful lump to her throat.

It bore the insignia of a still popular local surf shop and Alex had often worn it in the old days. If she was truly in command of herself and the situation she'd make some joking comment about his shirt almost being an heirloom.

It used to be a favourite of his. And of hers. She used to slide her arms around him, rub her cheek on the soft material over his chest. She could almost feel the reassuring hardness of his body now—

'Is Niall here?' she asked instead, her perfidiously erotic thoughts adding an extra sharpness to her tone.

'Sure. Come in. We're just finishing a game.' Alex stood back and after a long moment Shea stepped reluctantly inside.

The floor was still covered in expensive Italian tiles, just as Shea remembered from the one time she'd visited the house, the night of Patti Rosten's eighteenth birthday party. At the time she vowed she'd never set foot in the place again. And once again she'd been forced by circumstances to break a pledge to herself.

Now the magnificent entry was lined with scaffolding, and drop-sheets covered parts of the tiled floor. One side of the high walls had already been painted a clear light beige, a far more pleasing colour than the heavy ochre shade it had been.

The deep mahogany staircase curved up to the left but Alex motioned that she precede him down a wide hall to the right.

'Mind all the paraphernalia,' Alex remarked from behind her, far too close behind her. 'I can't wait to get the painting finished and lighten the place. The dark colours are too oppressive and I never felt they did the house justice.'

Shea thought the same but she refrained from agreeing with him. Her steps paused as they approached the first open doorway and she lowered her voice.

'Niall was supposed to be home by six o'clock and he's usually very good about curfews. We...I was beginning to worry.'

'I know.'

Shea gave him a sharp look.

'I just rang Norah to reassure her I'd be dropping the boys home. She said you were on your way.' Alex motioned towards the open door and, feeling even more disgruntled, Shea could only step down into what was obviously now a huge rumpus room.

If Shea remembered correctly it used to be a large and very opulent dining room that would seat dozens of people. Alex's stereo and television equipment was now set in between bookshelves that lined one entire wall. Stacked in one corner were unpacked boxes, presumably full of books to go on the shelves.

The boys were standing beside a full-sized pool table, Pete leaning across to make his shot. The balls clicked and with a clacking thud one fell into a pocket.

'Oh, no. You sank it.' Niall groaned. 'You're slaughtering me.' He turned and saw his mother and his face lit up. 'Hi, Mum! Look at this pool table. Isn't it excellent? Alex has been giving Pete and me a few tips. Want to have a go?'

'No. Not tonight,' Shea made herself say easily. 'It's almost dinner time and I've come to give you and Pete a lift home.'

'You needn't have done that. Alex was going to drive us in his Jag. Hey, maybe he still could and then he can stay to dinner.'

Shea's green eyes slid sideways and met Alex's apparently guileless gaze.

'I'm sure Gran wouldn't mind,' Niall was continuing, 'and she always cooks plenty of stuff.'

'I'd love the chance to re-acquaint myself with Norah's cooking,' Alex said lightly.

I'm sure you would, Shea wanted to scream at him. He knew she didn't want to see him and he was just trying to goad her.

'However, I'm afraid I can't tonight, Niall. I have another engagement.'

Shea blinked in amazement. Another engagement? She only just prevented herself from asking him where he was going.

'Aw, gee, Alex. It would have been great if you could have come.' Niall frowned his disappointment.

'There'll be plenty of other nights. Perhaps Alex can make it some other time.' Shea hoped she'd put more sincerity into the invitation than she felt, although the tightening of Alex's mouth implied she hadn't deceived him in the least.

'Come and have a quick look over the house while the boys are finishing their game,' he suggested cursorily enough.

'Yes, Mum. The house is humungous,' Niall told her. 'And the view's extremely excellent.'

Shea hesitated.

'Come on. It won't take long.' Alex took her elbow and Shea immediately moved away from him, towards the door.

Her movement seemed to be taken as read that she wanted a guided tour of Alex's mansion. Which she didn't, she told herself angrily. She just wanted to go home.

'Along the hallway to the right,' Alex indicated and Shea could only follow his directions. 'I haven't changed much in the way of the floor plan. My major problem was with the decor.'

They looked at the large kitchen which seemed to feature every labour-saving device Shea could imagine. It used to be dark, Shea recalled, but Alex had replaced the old brown counter-tops with bright rich cream ones that contrasted with the dark stained wood of the cupboard doors. The floor was light now, too, and the room open and inviting.

The formal dining room and separate lounge featured a huge two-way stone fireplace and the carpet had been taken up to reveal polished wooden floors now covered by a few thick scatter rugs. It was, Shea acknowledged, now more a home than a showplace.

They walked up the curved staircase and Shea moved quickly from one bedroom to another. It was obvious which room was Alex's. The suit he'd worn earlier hung on a hanger on the closet door and a light pullover was draped over the end of the king-sized bed.

Shea took all this in as she popped her head in the doorway and she was about to continue on but Alex's body behind her effectively blocked her exit.

'This room has the best view, I think. Come and have a look,' he said levelly and Shea walked across the thick pile of the carpet to step out through the sliding doors onto the balcony.

Alex was right. The view was wonderful, and the cool evening breeze lifted some loose strands of Shea's hair to tease the side of her cheek.

Every muscle in Shea's body tensed and she gasped a shallow breath. 'I was going to come and see you.' She said the very first thing that unscrambled in her mind.

'About the lease,' she added quickly in case he misinterpreted her statement.

'I thought Aston was handling all that.' The rough angles of his face set in the dusky light. 'However, as I said before, I'd prefer to talk directly to you.' His brown eyes held hers.

'I don't see why you'd need to but—' She shrugged, wishing she could tell him to forget it and just walk away. However, the truth of the matter, she told herself once again, was that it would be bad business to jeopardise the leasing of the building just because she didn't care for the building's owner. And she prided herself on being a good businesswoman.

She lifted her chin. 'I'm quite prepared to negotiate with you over the terms. I'll be at the shop all day tomorrow if you want to drop by,' she added, the words almost sticking in her throat.

'Thank you,' he acknowledged drily. 'I might just do that.'

Shea broke his gaze and turned to look at the view again. The bay curved below them and from their high vantage point the coastline stretched northwards, a picturesque mixture of dark green foliage, a light cream ribbon of sand and the darkening water tinged with gold as the setting sun was about to dip behind the low mountains to the west. A couple of sailboard riders still braved the waves even at this late hour.

'Do you remember that beach?' Alex asked huskily, the intimacy of his tone making Shea turn sharply to glance at him.

'The beach?' she repeated, her own voice thin and strained as her tongue threatened to stick to the top of her suddenly dry mouth. Of course she remembered. How could she forget? But she would have taken bets that he had.

'We spent a lot of time down there,' he added huskily. 'Do you remember?'

'Yes.' She swallowed convulsively. She remembered it all. The good times. And the bad. 'It was a long time ago, Alex,' she declared testily and moved a few steps away from him, resting her palms on the wrought-iron railings, needing the solid support.

The view was even more impressive from where she now stood but Shea had difficulty focusing on it. She was far too conscious of Alex's hard body so close behind her. And she sensed rather than heard him take a few steps nearer, narrowing the distance between them again.

He was beside her now and the fine hairs on her arms stood to attention as his elbow brushed her skin.

'I always associate the sound of the sea with you.' His deep voice flowed over her. 'With us.'

CHAPTER SEVEN

SHEA'S fingers tightened painfully on the ironwork of the railing, its pitted surface biting into her soft flesh. The repetitive crash of the surf, the cascade of the receding water on the sand, the harsh cries of the gulls faded into the gathering twilight. The sounds were drowned out by his lowly spoken words.

'*I always associate the sound of the sea with you.*'

So do I with you, she wanted to shout at him.

He couldn't know that for years she'd taken back streets so she wouldn't have to drive along the length of that bay, so she wouldn't have to see the trees, the sand, the white caps racing across the blue water, so she wouldn't have to feel the salty dampness of the breeze.

But of course she hadn't been able to make detours around her dreams. When she'd closed her eyes at night memories of Alex had returned to torture her.

'I'd remember the way the sunlight burned your hair almost white.' Alex's deep voice continued washing over her and she felt a glow of heat suffuse her body. 'I'd remember losing myself in the green depths of your eyes.'

He'd turned his head and his warm breath fanned her hair, her sensitive earlobe, and waves of erotic sensations broke over her. 'And in my dreams I felt the softness of your body in my arms, tasted the salt of the sea on your skin.'

'Alex, please—' Shea tried to step away from him, put the rationality of space between them, but her legs seemed to be paralysed, refused to take her direction.

'I haunted your dreams, too, didn't I?' His hoarsely murmured words betrayed his own arousal and the eroticism of them taunted her.

'Didn't I, Shea?'

A burst of purely physical wanting exploded inside her and she clutched frantically at the railings. She wanted to throw herself into his arms, pull off his sweatshirt, run her lips over the smoothness of his chest, feel his hard body against hers.

'Alex, don't do this to me,' she pleaded brokenly, feeling the dampness of tears on her face as she turned to face him.

Their eyes met, held, and the atmosphere about them came alive with undiluted sensuality. Alex moved as if in slow motion, leant forward, until his oh so familiar mouth claimed hers.

And Shea made no move to deflect that kiss. In fact, she rather suspected she swayed to meet him. Only their lips touched. Parted. Touched again. And Shea's heartbeats thundered, wildly tempestuous in her breast. Eleven years slipped away in split seconds.

And his lips weren't enough. She needed so much more. She wanted his arms around her. She craved the heady feeling of his hardness against her. She yearned for him to be part of her, the way he used to be.

'Mum? Alex? Where are you?' Niall's young voice slowly penetrated the torrent of desire that held Shea in its seductive deluge.

And even then she was slow to move, to break the grip of the intoxicating passion that seemed to have control of them both. With a low moan she put her hand on Alex's chest, pushed almost feebly against him, and made herself step away from him as she turned to face her son.

'We thought you'd gone and got lost,' Niall said easily as he stood just inside the bedroom, looking out at them through the open sliding doors.

Had Niall seen them? Shea wondered as she strained to see his face in the darkness of the room. And if he had, what was he thinking?

'Finished the game?' Alex asked him with equal nonchalance. 'Who won?'

Niall shrugged resignedly. 'Pete. I think he's a natural. I'm really going to have to get some practice.'

'I guess we should be going.' Shea stepped off the patio and into the bedroom, flinching as Alex reached inside to flick on the light. The brightness made her even more aware of her heated body and she felt her cheeks begin to colour anew under her son's gaze. 'Your grandmother will be wondering where we are,' she said as lightly as she could as she made herself walk through the door and start down the steps.

'Gran knows we're with Alex,' Niall said casually, as though being with Alex was something they did every day.

'Well, Pete's mother might be worrying.'

'Oh, she knows I'm with Niall and Alex,' Pete Gavin said from the bottom of the steps. 'No sweat, Mrs Finlay.'

At the front door Shea paused, turned to face Alex, her eyes sliding from his face to the safety of the tiled floor. 'Thank you for putting up with the boys,' she began. 'I hope they weren't, I mean, I hope they didn't hold you up too much. With the painting and, well, everything,' Shea finished breathily.

'They weren't any trouble.' Alex rested one strong arm on the door jamb as Shea hustled the boys out onto the step. 'Come any time,' he said with easy ambiguity, the expression in his eyes telling her his invitation wasn't just extended to the boys.

Shea's pulse gave a jolt and she almost bolted for the car. And her heartbeats were still racing as she thankfully turned out of the driveway and onto the road.

Dinner was a great strain for Shea. She had to force down each morsel of food and no matter how hard she tried she couldn't seem to erase the feel of Alex's kiss from her mind. Or the feel of it from her mouth. She felt as though the imprint of his lips glowed iridescently for all the world to see.

Niall appeared to Shea to be a little quieter than usual. However, she told herself that she was imagining things, because of her guilty conscience. If Niall had seen her kissing Alex then no doubt he would talk to her about it. Niall was nothing if not open and straightforward. At least he always had been.

Eventually they had finished their meal and Niall went off to do his homework. Pete was coming over, Niall told Shea, so they could tackle a particularly difficult lot of mathematics. So Shea sat with Norah and watched a little television. But of course the shows couldn't hold her interest. Her thoughts kept sliding irrepressibly back to Alex.

When the show came to an end Norah looked up from her tapestry and Shea thankfully went to switch off the television set.

'Did you want to watch something else?' Shea asked and Norah shook her head.

'Oh, dear.' Norah berated herself. 'I forgot to tell you David Aston rang while you were collecting Niall. He said he'll drop by the shop tomorrow. Something about a lease.'

Shea shifted uncomfortably. She hadn't exactly taken advantage of her time with Alex to discuss business. In fact after their initial dialogue about the lease all thoughts of Alex's stand-off about it had simply slipped from her mind. Such was the force of Alex's hold on her, she chastised herself silently. The building and her business couldn't have been further from her mind when Alex kissed her.

'Business discussions,' she said with mock derision. 'Sounds like another boring day at the office.' She feigned a yawn. 'I think I'll have an early night to prepare myself.'

Norah smiled. 'That'll do you the world of good, love. I'll see you in the morning.'

Shea had a quick shower and stopped by to say good-night to Niall and Pete, spending a little time with them commiserating over their homework. Then she escaped guiltily to her room. She wasn't in the least tired but she needed to be by herself. To think about Alex. And her disastrous reaction to him.

She lay back against her pillows and sighed. Her behaviour this evening had been reprehensible. She'd allowed her physical vulnerability to overcome her steadfast resolutions. And she couldn't allow that to happen again. She was a grown woman now and certainly couldn't hide behind the excuse of youth for her foolishness. There was no way, she decided determinedly, that she was going to give Alex Finlay the power to break her heart again.

Very impressive after the fact, and away from Alex, she told herself disparagingly. The truth was that Alex's kiss had swept away the ensuing years with almost indecent ease. The second his lips had claimed hers she had become that naïve, infatuated teenager, her body straining for the satisfaction only he could give her, but now her responses were completely, disconcertingly adult.

In her own defence she reminded herself she had been a widow for four years. She was ripe for any physical contact, wasn't she? Alex's arrival had simply been perfect timing.

David Aston has been available for months and she hadn't been even remotely tempted, a small voice inside her reminded her with a ruthless lack of compassion.

No, she told herself. It was a matter of coincidence. The right place, the right time.

The right man, suggested that same inner voice, and Shea groaned softly.

Standing there with Alex on the balcony that overlooked that particular beach had been a mistake and Shea had known that from the moment she stepped out there. The beach below them held so many memories for her, memories of Alex. Especially the night of Patti Rosten's birthday party.

Patti was visiting Byron Bay with her father who had bought the big white house that was quite a local landmark. Being a year older than Shea and, by all accounts, a seasoned world traveller, Patti was welcomed into their group with more than a little admiration.

That Alex Finlay had introduced her to everyone only added to Patti's easy acceptance. Joe Rosten and Alex's father were old army buddies and Donald Finlay had asked his son to take young Patti under his wing.

From the first time Shea met Patti she recognised that the other girl was not unimpressed by Alex's good looks and Shea knew she was gripped by what she told herself was an understandable jealousy. What disturbed Shea was Patti's blatant obviousness. She used every opportunity to clutch simperingly at Alex's arm or to gaze up at him with openly adoring eyes.

So when the party invitation arrived Shea was less than enthusiastic. However, Norah had emphasised that Patti was a stranger to the district, a visitor to Australia, and Shea had eventually agreed to go.

On the day of the party she had phoned Alex all afternoon without success. She had forgotten to ask him what time he intended collecting her to take her to the big white house.

And when Jamie arrived home to inform her that Alex had spent the best part of the day over at the Rosten's helping them prepare for the party she had felt a surge of renewed resentment.

'Alex also asked me to drive you to the party and he'll see you there,' Jamie added. 'He said he'd barely have time to race home and change.'

So it was with no little disquiet that Shea had walked up the steps of the big white house in the company of Jamie and his date for the party. They were shown through to the back of the house which opened out onto a large courtyard overlooking a huge swimming pool. Coloured lights had been strung up everywhere and there were about sixty or so young people already there.

To Shea's further dismay Patti walked across to greet them with Alex by her side.

Patti wore the tightest pair of designer jeans Shea had ever seen and her thin sleeveless tank top, made of some gold shimmery material, accentuated the curve of her small breasts. Her dark hair had been styled onto the top of her head and she looked so much older than her eighteen years.

Shea's heart sank. Patti's appearance made Shea feel very passé in her patterned wraparound skirt and sleeveless blouse.

'How wonderful of you to come,' she said to them, her large violet eyes fringed by thick dark lashes looking up at the man beside her. 'Isn't it, Alex?'

'It sure is.' Alex grinned at Shea and took her hand. 'Come on and I'll get you a drink.'

'Happy birthday, Patti.' Shea handed the other girl a gaily wrapped present.

'Oh. Thanks, Shea.' Patti turned slightly and put her hand on Alex's arm. 'Get me a drink, too, will you, Sugar.'

'Sugar?' Shea repeated softly to Alex as they crossed to a bar that had been set up off to the right and Alex laughed softly.

'Not my favourite form of address, even with someone I know well.'

'And you don't know Patti well, do you?' Shea asked as lightly as she could.

'Not that well.' He glanced down at Shea. 'I'm sorry about not picking you up tonight. I was here all afternoon and Dad and Joe kept me pretty busy.'

Patti, too, Shea reflected silently.

The night wore slowly on and it seemed to Shea that Patti always found something for Alex to do to separate him from Shea. That set the tone of the evening for Shea and she had a perfectly wretched time. Patti interrupted when Alex and Shea were dancing, when they were talking to friends and even when they stood enjoying the delicious supper that was provided.

By eleven o'clock Shea knew she couldn't bear it a moment longer and she sought Alex out and asked him to take her home.

Alex set down the bag of ice he was carrying and glanced at his wristwatch. 'It's still early. Sure you want to go?'

'I can ask Jamie to drop me home if you want to stay longer,' Shea suggested with a sinking heart.

'No. It's okay. We can go. I'll just get rid of this ice and then we can make our goodbyes.'

Shea followed Alex over to the bar and watched him add the ice to the soft drink tub. Of course Patti materialised from nowhere.

'Thanks, Alex, Sugar. What would I have done without you today?'

Alex grinned wryly. 'You wouldn't have had any trouble getting half a dozen other guys to do it instead. Anyway, Shea's feeling tired so we'll say goodnight and thanks for inviting us.'

Patti's full lips pouted. 'There's no need for you to go if Shea's tired, is there? Maybe you can come back when you've dropped Shea home.'

'Maybe.' Alex took his car keys from his pocket and with a minimum of fuss they were outside and he was unlocking his car.

'You can go back if you want to,' Shea said thickly as she slid into the passenger seat.

'Not likely,' Alex said firmly. 'Patti's a spoilt little minx, used to getting her own way, and that can be very wearing. Dad volunteered my services today and I think I've done my share. And apart from that I haven't had a chance to spend enough time with you tonight.' He set the car in motion and reached across to clasp her hand.

Shea sighed. 'I've had a perfectly awful evening because I thought you, well, wanted to be with Patti rather than me.'

'Are you kidding? If it hadn't been Patti's birthday I wouldn't have even gone. You know I hate parties, unless there's just the two of us.'

'Me, too.' Shea smiled and began to feel just a little better. 'I'm not really tired. Just tired of the party. Can we go for a walk on the beach?'

'Sure can.' Alex squeezed her hand and then concentrated on manoeuvering the car down the winding road.

They had walked hand in hand along the beach, the lights of the party visible high above them, but the repetitive crash of the waves drowned out the celebratory sounds. Eventually they retraced their steps but instead of taking the track that led up to the car Shea stopped and took hold of Alex's arm.

'Let's sit here for a while. The beach is so lovely at night. Isn't the view unreal? The moon's so bright and it's so romantic.'

Alex held the luminous dial of his wristwatch to the moonlight. 'It's getting late, Shea. Norah will be expecting me to get you home.'

'I know. But a little while won't hurt, will it? Come on, Alex. Please,' she appealed, turning to uninhibitedly slide her arms around his waist, her fingertips unconsciously luxuriating in the feel of firm muscle beneath his light shirt.

His hands went to rest on her shoulders and his thumbs gently rubbed her collarbone. Shea shivered, the sound of his fingers on the cloth of her sleeveless top magnifying sensually in her ears.

'Aren't you cold in that thin shirt?' he asked softly, his eyes running over her, and she shook her head, moving closer to him, resting her cheek against his chest, breathing in the intoxicating smell that was so totally his.

Her heartbeats went mad and she snuggled closer, and his arms slid back around her, folding her to him.

'I missed you this afternoon. No one seemed to know where you were.'

'I'm sorry we got our wires crossed. I should have called you myself to explain that Dad and Joe expected me to help with the preparations.'

'Well, I understand now. Oh, Alex, hold me,' she whispered, her breath caught in her suddenly constricted throat. 'Make love to me.'

'Shea.' For a moment his arms tightened and then his hands went to her upper arms, moving her slightly away from him. 'Shea, come on. I told you we can't get into that because—' He stopped and sighed.

'Because I'm too young,' she finished, her frustration adding a mocking note to her voice. 'And I've told you before I'm not too young. I'm seventeen, you know.'

'And I'm nearly twenty-two, Shea. Old enough to know better.'

Shea suppressed a chuckle, her nerve endings still jangling excitedly. 'Twenty-two's about due for your first walking stick,' she teased, and Alex smiled, the moonlight playing over his features. Along his square jaw, insinuating in the creases bracketing his mouth, sliding over his high cheekbones, sparkling incitingly in his eyes that were black now beneath his lashes.

She gazed up at him and her heart shifted peculiarly in her breast.

'I love you,' she whispered huskily and she heard him catch his breath.

She also felt tension take hold of him and she stood on tiptoe to touch her lips to his.

The softness of her tentative caress seemed to hold him motionless for long seconds before he pulled her against him, his mouth hardening on hers until they clung together, hearts racing in unison.

Then Alex was drawing away from her and she tightened her arms feverishly around his neck, her firm breasts hard against his chest.

'Shea, we have to stop this,' he said thickly. 'You don't know what you're doing...'

'Only what I always want to do, what I can hardly stop myself from doing when I'm with you. Oh, Alex, please tell me you feel the same.'

'I do. But, hell, Shea, I'm older and it's my responsibility to...' His fingers tightened painfully as his gaze burned down on her. 'But I like the feel of you in my arms far too much,' he finished huskily and he gave her one quick sharp kiss before setting her apart from him.

Shea brushed a strand of fair hair back from her face and sighed. 'You feel good in my arms, too,' she told him, and he grimaced, taking her hand and starting them walking again along the path that led back to the car. 'You always do.' She smiled happily.

'Shea!' His voice held a frown but his lips were smiling.

'Well, you do. We sort of fit together. And besides, it's different with you, Alex.'

He chuckled. 'Different from what? Or should I say, whom?'

'From anyone else,' Shea stated easily.

'I see. What have you been up to while I've been away playing football?' He sounded amused but Shea felt the pressure of his fingers increase around her hand and she shrugged.

'I let one of the guys at the school dance kiss me goodnight. Well, two guys, actually. Not both at once, one at a time,' she added honestly.

Alex paused, his eyelashes falling, narrowing his eyes to mere dark slashes in the shadowy moonlight.

'It was awful. Both times,' she told him with feeling.

He began walking again. 'Shea, that's what I mean. You're young. You've got it all before you. Going out with plenty of boys your own age.'

'Ugh! Boys is the operative word.' Shea sighed loudly, hanging back so Alex was forced to stop. 'They bore me to death. All they can talk about is their bomby old cars. And they're, well, they're sloppy kissers. Yuck!'

'That's not very flattering.' Alex laughed and shook his head in mock exasperation. 'What am I going to do with you, Shea Stanley?'

Shea stepped closer to him, leaned against his hard chest. 'If I told you it would be X-rated.'

Alex's fingers lifted her chin and he grinned down at her. 'My! My! Now that sounds positively decadent.'

'You're laughing at me.' Shea frowned. 'Why can't you see that I'm all grown up?' Her hand reached up to cup his slightly beard-roughened jaw line.

'You,' he said with mock sternness, 'are one persistent little baggage. Let's walk.'

They started up the steep part of the track, climbing in silence until they came to the last and steepest section.

'Let me go first and then I'll pull you up,' Alex said, his joggers slipping on the sandy bank. 'Someone should build some wooden steps for this part of the track.'

'Then everyone would come down here and it wouldn't be our secret place anymore.' Shea took Alex's hand and he hoisted her over the top of the bank.

'Mind your step.' He turned as he held back an overhanging branch and at that moment the toe of Shea's sandal caught on a tree root and she stumbled forward, Alex's strong arms catching her as she fell.

'Are you all right?' he asked as he set her down and she laughed softly.

'I'm fine. Just a tangle foot.' She moved her hands over his back, her fingers finding the indentation of his backbone beneath his shirt. 'Mmmm. Did I tell you this close you feel divine?'

And the top two buttons of his shirt had sprung open, inviting her to slide her lips over his skin, her tongue tip teasing the hollow at the base of his throat.

'Shea!'

She slid one hand around and deftly undid the rest of the buttons, her fingers darting inside his shirt to slither playfully over his ribcage, up into the light mat of soft hair on his chest, circling one instantaneously aroused male nipple.

'Shea, please! Do you know what you're inviting?'

'Mmmm!' she breathed huskily, her lips and fingertips sensuously caressing.

Alex's hands were unsteady as he cupped her face, lifting her head so that his mouth could claim hers. His kisses deepened, seared her, turned her legs to jelly, set spirals of fire radiating through her body like sparks driven by a winter westerly wind.

She moulded her body to his, her first realisation of his arousal making her light-headed. She moved instinctively against him and he pulled her sleeveless shirt from the waistband of her skirt, his fingers sliding up beneath it to envelop her full breasts which seemed to swell at his exquisite touch.

Shea had never experienced anything like the depth of feeling that took hold of her then. Or thought she hadn't. Until his fingers found the taut nipples, one and then the other, and she moaned deliriously, scarcely daring to believe his touch could feel so earth-shatteringly sensational.

'Shea. Shea.' He murmured her name and then took a deep ragged breath, fighting for control. Then he straightened her shirt. 'Do you realise anyone could come walking down this track?' he began, and Shea swallowed a throaty laugh.

'No one ever comes along here. Except a crab or two. And us.' She took his hand and pulled him after her up the grassy bank off the track, ducking beneath the screening overhanging leaves of a low tree.

'No one can see us now.' She turned back to him. 'If you look through the gap there you can see the sea. I found this one day and I come here sometimes when I want to be alone.' She rained light kisses along his jaw up to his earlobe. 'Welcome to my special place, my very special person.'

'Oh, Shea.' His lips trailed fire over her throat, down the valley between her breasts, only to be stopped by the low neckline of her top. Without pausing he lifted it over her head and let it fall to the ground.

Shea slipped his open shirt from his shoulders and when he unclipped her bra, freeing her breasts, she heard him catch his breath.

'You are so beautiful,' he said slowly, the deep fluid tone of his voice playing over her skin like liquid silk, and she lifted his hands to her body that burned for him, for only him.

Desire rose in her, almost choking her and when she spoke her own voice broke achingly, sounding so unlike her own as she repeated her earlier entreaty.

'Alex, please. Make love to me.'

CHAPTER EIGHT

His hands went to her naked breasts, alabaster in the tree-shaded moonlight, his fingers gently teasing, tantalising, destroying every last vestige of her control with consummate ease.

She moaned his name and somehow they had sunk to their knees, then were lying side by side on the sand, the moonlight that filtered through the leafy canopy dancing patterns across their exposed skin.

Alex's mouth trailed from hers, over her chin, her throat, his lips slowly climbing the mound of her breast, his tongue tip encircling the sharp rosy peak before capturing its summit, causing mind-shattering, so erotic sensations to tumble over her like a cascading waterfall.

Shea's fingers twined in his curling fair hair, binding him to her. His hand moved downwards to cup her hip, rose to impatiently untie the band of her wraparound skirt, continued downwards again, sliding over her thigh, rising, fingers splayed across her buttocks beneath the thin bikini pants she wore.

On a wave of impetuous longing Shea's own fingers fumbled to undo the buckle of his belt.

'Shea, no! We've got to cool down.'

The zip of his jeans rasped downwards. 'But I want to touch you, too,' she whispered thickly, peeling away the soft scrub-washed denim. And as her hands gently, eagerly, found their target he groaned impassionedly, burying his lips between her breasts.

'Shea, please. I want you so much. Do you know how hard it is for me to hold back?'

Her fingers caressed him lovingly. 'I don't want you to stop, Alex. I love you. Please love me, too.'

'I do love you. So much. Shea, I don't think I...' His mouth crushed hers and his hands slipped her pants down, returning to the soft curl-covered mound to show her even more wondrous delights.

Shea arched towards him and when he slid over her she met him without restraint, her initial cry of pain muffled in his mouth as he claimed her. She stiffened momentarily and he stroked her face, murmured incomprehensibly to her so that when he began to move inside her she relaxed with him, her pain forgotten in the joy of being one with him.

Afterwards they lay together in silence, legs still entwined, and Shea wearily ran her finger over the tanned bulging muscles in his arm. Alex lifted himself from her, separating them, and the breeze blew chillingly on her damp skin.

She clutched at him. 'Alex, don't go.'

'Ssh!' he soothed softly, settling her into the crook of his arm, her head resting on his shoulder. 'I'm not going. I haven't the strength just yet,' he added derisively, his fingers brushing the damp tendrils of hair back from her forehead. 'Did I hurt you badly?'

She shook her head, running her lips over his salty skin, tasting him. 'Only a little at first. It was...' She swallowed unevenly. 'It was beautiful.'

'Beautiful. Like you,' he agreed throatily, kissing her temple.

They lay together until their breathing had slowed and then Alex sighed.

'Shea, I feel like a bloody heel for...'

She silenced him with her finger on his lips. 'No. Don't spoil it, Alex, please. It wasn't your fault. I love you and I wanted you to make love to me. Desperately. I have for ages. I...was it...? Did you...?'

He ran his hand lingeringly over her breast and she felt a renewal of the now familiar delightful tingle of wanting rise inside her.

'It was and I did, my love.' He smiled down at her.

'X-rated?' Shea asked with a husky chuckle and he lifted her on top of him, gazing adoringly up at her.

'Oh, Shea.' He closed his eyes emotively and then rolled them over, stretching out his length beside her, raising himself on his elbow. 'I can see I'm going to have my hands full with you over the next sixty years or so, Shea Stanley.'

His hands, of their own accord, reached out to cup the curve of her cheek and he slowly lowered his head, blocking out most of Shea's light, finding her lips with his, kissing her druggingly before moving his mouth downwards to tantalise, to so easily arouse her once more, her senses surging to his touch.

'So very beautiful.' His voice seemed to catch in his throat and his breath teased her still sensitive nipples before he took one and then the other in his mouth.

Desire rose to race through her again and she laughed a little embarrassedly. 'Am I really beautiful?'

Alex looked into her eyes. 'You're simply perfect, my love.'

His lips returned to nuzzle her breast and Shea moaned softly.

'We should be getting home. Norah will be worried about you.'

'No she won't. She knows I'm with you.'

Alex paused, ran a hand over the line of his jaw. 'That doesn't make me feel better somehow.'

'What do you mean?'

'I mean, Norah trusts me to take care of you. I haven't done such a great job tonight.'

'Yes, you have.'

Alex shook his head. 'We didn't take precautions and that's not sensible or responsible.'

'Don't you want to have children?'

'Of course I do. But not yet. You're too young to tie yourself down. You need time to enjoy yourself.'

'You mean we won't do this again?'

'We shouldn't. But I don't trust myself not to. Not now.' He kissed her again. 'Next time I'll be prepared.'

But the damage had been done. Shea grimaced to herself. No, not damage, she told herself. Niall was the best thing that had happened to her in the mess she'd made of her life back then. He'd been the reason she'd kept going during that dreadful time after Alex had left, abandoning her.

Yet as Niall had grown from babyhood she'd clutched to her the bittersweet pleasure that he was so much like Alex. Like his father.

Shea shifted guiltily, knowing Jamie had been all and more than a father to her son. He'd been the one to hear Niall's first word, see Niall take his first step, watch Niall play his first soccer game. All these unique milestones should have been experienced by Alex. If he'd wanted to be part of them.

That was the operative ingredient, she told herself. If Alex had wanted to share them. Which he hadn't.

Because she hadn't given him the chance, a harsh voice inside reminded her, and for the first time in years hot tears rose in her eyes and overflowed onto her cheeks. Shea angrily dashed them away.

What could she have said back then? she asked herself. Alex had made up his mind to leave, to follow his ambitions. A wife and child would have held him back. He'd implied as much.

She lay back in her bed and when she finally fell into an uneasy sleep her pillow was damp with her tears.

*   *   *

After her restless night Shea was almost pleased when it was time to get out of bed and dress. She chose one of her own mix-and-match designs, a khaki skirt and short-sleeved jacket, coupled with a soft blouse in complimenting grey-green tones.

She had barely set the coffee pot perking when Niall came in and sat down.

'You're early this morning,' she said with some surprise. Usually they had to badger him to get out of bed.

Niall yawned. 'Mmmm. Guess I was hungry.'

'How hungry?' Shea asked. 'Cereal and toast hungry or bacon and eggs hungry?'

'Just cereal, thanks, Mum. I can get it.' Niall walked over to the pantry and chose his favourite cereal, tipping a large serving into a bowl.

Shea set a glass of orange juice on the table for him and gave him a hug as he sat down.

'What was that for?' he asked, hugging her back.

'Just for good morning.'

He poured milk on his cereal and took a couple of spoonfuls as Shea sat down opposite him and began to butter her toast.

'Mum?'

She looked up and Niall gave her a level look.

'You remember the other night we were talking about you going out with guys and stuff? Well, have you never really thought about getting married again?'

Shea raised her eyebrows in surprise. 'No, I haven't. Not really.'

'I guess you loved Dad a lot, hey?'

'Yes, I did.' Shea made herself continue spreading strawberry jam on her toast.

'Is that why you've never wanted to marry anyone else?'

'Partly. I suppose I haven't really had much time to think about it.'

'But if you meet someone, someone really nice, you would want to, wouldn't you?'

'I suppose I would,' she agreed carefully.

'I mean, when I grow up and get a house of my own you and Gran will be all alone.'

'I hope you're not planning on leaving just yet,' Shea tried to lighten the sensitive subject and Niall gave her a censorious frown.

'Of course not. Be serious, Mum,' he admonished, and Shea sighed, knowing she wasn't going to divert the subject when Niall was in his 'man of the family' mode.

'I don't feel I want to remarry just yet. But if I met someone I loved very much, I would. How does that sound?'

'I wouldn't mind having a stepfather,' Niall told her solemnly. 'And I know you wouldn't marry just anybody, Mum.'

'Thank you,' Shea put in succinctly as Niall continued.

'You wouldn't marry someone like the guy Mike Leary's mother married. Mike says his stepfather's a real dork. But I know you'd pick someone nice.'

'Niall—'

'I know we talked about him the other night but, what do you really think of David Aston?' he asked, serious enquiry in the expression on his young face.

'David and I are just friends and I've no intention of taking it any further. I've told you that already, Niall. Which makes me wonder why you'd even consider it. I thought you didn't like him.'

'I don't much. I told you he's a wimp and, besides that, he makes out he really likes me when you're around. He's a crawler.'

'Niall, I don't think—'

'Well, he does.'

'Niall,' Shea reiterated firmly. 'You shouldn't be talking about David like that. It's really quite rude.'

'I'd only say it to you, Mum. Honest.' His eyes dropped to focus on his breakfast as he absently moved his spoon, drawing circles in his cereal. 'Alex isn't a wimp,' he said casually.

Shea's mouth went suddenly dry and she swallowed quickly. 'Niall—'

'Alex is pretty great,' Niall continued hurriedly. 'I like him a lot. And I just wanted to, well, I wanted you to know that.'

Shea's gaze held her son's. 'Look, Niall. Alex is your father's cousin and he's, he was, a friend of mine and your father's. But that was a long time ago. People change and—' Shea swallowed again. 'I don't want you to think that, well, that anything—'

'I saw you last night,' Niall said quickly. 'With Alex. Sucking face.'

'Sucking—?' Shea spluttered. 'Niall! That's a dreadful expression.'

'That's what the kids at school call it.' He grinned. 'It is awful, isn't it? But I did see you kissing Alex and I thought,' Niall shrugged his thin shoulders, 'I just thought that maybe you kind of liked Alex, too.'

'Look, Niall,' Shea began carefully. 'Sometimes adults kiss each other for other reasons besides the . . . I mean, kissing someone doesn't have to mean you want to get involved with them.'

Niall nodded. 'I know that, Mum. But I wouldn't mind at all, if you and Alex, you know, did decide to get involved.'

'Oh, Niall.' Shea ran a hand through her still loose hair. 'I can understand that you like Alex but you can't just, well, just organise things or people to be the way you want them to be.'

Niall sighed heavily.

'And, Niall,' Shea added reproachfully. 'Please don't discuss this with anyone else, will you?'

'No, I won't. But if you and Alex—'

'Niall!' Shea cautioned her son sharply. 'Alex and I haven't seen each other since before you were born. We're all but strangers, so let's just leave it. OK?' Shea held up her hand when Niall would have commented. 'And don't pressure me about it either or else I'll think you're just looking for an excuse to have a party,' Shea finished, trying to add a lightness to her tone she was far from feeling.

Now, sitting at her desk, a pile of invoices before her, Shea almost groaned as she went over her conversation with her son. Niall had always been a friendly child but she'd never known him to become as easily and quickly interested in anyone as he had with Alex and it disturbed her greatly.

Perhaps, as Norah had said, Niall needed a father figure in his life, a male who was closer to his family than his teachers at school. That was quite feasible, she told herself rationally. But that Alex should fill that role!

Shea's fingers tightened on her pen as fear clutched at her. Although what she was most afraid of she couldn't quite sort out. She knew she was terrified that Alex might suspect that Niall was his son. And if he did find out would he try to erode her son's affections from herself? Was Alex capable of that? In the beginning she would have said no, but now?

Shea set down her pen and rubbed at the beginnings of a headache that throbbed behind her eyes.

Niall had said he hoped that his mother might like Alex, too. But like? Like was hardly a word to use with Alex. It was far too insipid somehow. Adored? Worshipped? Idolised? Eleven years ago they all would have applied. And yes, she'd liked him as a person, too. But not now.

She'd barely given herself the chance to like him, that same persistent voice inside her criticised. Because she

had no wish to start it all over again, get involved, get
hurt.

Irritated with herself she picked up a sheaf of invoices
and was about to try to get her mind back on her work
when there was a tentative tap on her office door.

'Shea?' Debbie opened the door a fraction and poked
her head inside. 'Sorry to interrupt you but there's
someone to see you.' Debbie rolled her eyes impres-
sively. 'Alex Finlay.' She delivered his name in a tone
that seemed to demand the accompaniment of a fanfare
of trumpets.

Shea sat stunned for a few seconds before dropping
her eyes defensively to the invoices in her hand. 'Oh.
Yes. Well, tell him I'll be with him in a few moments,'
she said with as much detachment as she could, willing
herself not to blush in front of her young assistant.

'No hurry. I can wait.' Alex's deep voice made her
look up swiftly and she knew she'd failed to appear in-
different as heat washed her cheeks. Alex had gently
pushed the door fully open and his brown eyes steadily
held hers.

Shea swallowed quickly. 'Come in, Alex,' she said,
amazing herself at her business-like tone, and her
jangling nervous system stabilised a little.

'I'll make some coffee, shall I?' Debbie asked brightly
and Alex thanked her, turning his charming smile on the
other girl, causing Debbie to flush with pleasure as she
hurried off.

Alex closed the door and then casually leant back
against it. Today he'd forgone his business suit and wore
dark denim jeans and a pale green knit shirt. The short
sleeves of his shirt hugged his muscular biceps and the
soft material loosely moulded the contours of his broad
chest and flat midriff.

All this Shea took in as the silence between them
stretched blaringly.

Then Shea suddenly saw the two of them back on the balcony, warm bodies clinging tightly together, and her treacherous senses began their now familiar betrayal.

'May I sit down?' His voice, lowered to that arousing tone, cut into her outer composure and fed her inner apprehension.

He moved closer to her desk with a lack of discomfiture a small part of her couldn't but admire. How she hoped she was exuding such assurance. But he was indicating the chair beside the wall and she nodded.

'Of course,' she said quickly, her voice almost steady, and he lifted the chair closer to her desk, lowering himself into it with an unconsciously sensual grace.

Shea's heartbeats fluttered and she was thankful she'd chosen a blouse with a high collar, a collar that would hopefully conceal the tell-tale pulse that throbbed erratically at the base of her throat.

She knew she had to say something, defuse the heightened awareness that seemed to burgeon each time they met. But what? What could she say after last night? she asked herself desperately.

Wasn't attack the best form of defence? She took a steadying breath.

'Alex, before we start discussing the lease, I feel—' She swallowed painfully again. 'About last night. I feel I should apologise.'

'Apologise about what?' he asked with an unconcerned dispassion that sparked Shea's anger.

And she grasped gratefully at that wrath. It was so much easier to handle than that other far more dangerous emotion that hovered so threateningly close to the surface of her cool demeanour.

'I want to apologise for allowing the situation to get out of hand,' she replied, taking the direct approach. 'For letting the situation develop in the first place,' she elaborated tersely, and he shrugged.

'There were two people on that balcony last night, Shea,' he reminded her, his intonation bordering on indifference. 'Why take on the blame yourself?'

'Yes, well, regardless of where the blame is distributed, I feel I should make it quite clear that last night was a brief slip on my part and that you can rest assured that it won't happen again.'

The corners of Alex's mouth twisted into a brief wry smile. 'Pity. When we both enjoyed it so much.'

'You're very much mistaken,' Shea retorted indignantly.

'Mistaken about what? That we enjoyed it? Of course we enjoyed it,' he finished placatingly.

'Of course I didn't enjoy it,' Shea snapped at him. 'And in retrospect I'm extremely annoyed with myself for misleading you.'

Alex's dark brows rose eloquently. 'I don't think you mislead me at all.' A small smile played around his mouth and Shea stiffened irritatedly.

'Oh, for heaven's sake, Alex. If you're getting some perverse amusement out of this at my expense then you might as well go because I can assure you I'm far too busy to waste my time bandying coy innuendos with you.'

Alex straightened in the chair. 'Coy innuendos? That's almost emasculating,' he said lightly. 'And totally unreasonable considering I'm simply prepared to discuss this topic of your choice,' he finished with a mock grimace that only fanned Shea's once more rapidly rising rage.

However, she had to bite back any retort as Debbie chose that moment to tap on the door and enter carrying a tray containing two mugs of steaming coffee, a small milk jug and a matching sugar bowl.

Alex rose immediately to take it from her, and his easy smile discombobulated the young woman again.

'Thank you, Debbie,' Shea stated dryly, and with a quick sideways glance at her boss she hurriedly left them.

'Look, Alex,' Shea continued after the door had closed on them again and they each had their coffee, 'I'm trying to be rational about this.'

'Why?'

'Why? Because we're two adults and because, as you have reminded me before, we do have to see each other occasionally. I'm trying to make a difficult situation as uncomplicated as possible.'

Alex relaxed back in his chair, crossing one jean-clad leg over the other. 'Uncomplicated?' He gave a soft laugh. 'There's nothing uncomplicated about our situation, Shea, wouldn't you say?'

Shea's chest muscles tightened and she slowly moved her clasped hands to her lap, below the top of the desk, in case he saw the tension in her whitening knuckles. 'Things will only be complicated if we make them so,' she said with far more calmness than she was feeling. If Alex only knew just how complex everything was.

'The truth remains that we go back a long way, Shea. I can't forget that.' His brown eyes held hers. 'And after last night I don't think you can, either.'

He calmly raised his coffee mug to his lips and took an appreciative sip.

'I'm afraid you're labouring under a misapprehension.' Shea's nervous system was in tatters again and she desperately held on to her composure. 'Last night I, well, I'll admit I may have been carried away by the,' she swallowed quickly, 'by the view, the evening, perhaps a moment of romantic nostalgia. That doesn't mean I'm going to carry that unfortunate indiscretion over into the cold light of day.'

Alex's eyelashes fell, shielding the expression in his narrowed brown eyes as he regarded her silently for long moments. 'Perhaps you've changed more than I thought,' he said evenly. 'Back then you were at least honest.'

'Perhaps I'm simply not saying what you want to hear,' she suggested lightly and shrugged, shoving aside a frisson of guilt. 'And I am being honest, Alex. Why wouldn't I be?' she added defensively.

'Only you can answer that,' he said softly.

'I don't think this fencing with each other is getting us anywhere.' Shea pointedly picked up her pile of invoices. 'Let's leave it as is. There's been a lot of water flow under the bridge in eleven years.'

'That's a bit of a tired old cliché, isn't it?' Alex set his coffee mug on the desktop. 'What exactly am I to glean from it?'

'The obvious.' Shea shifted as casually as she could in her swivel chair. 'That we're not the same people we were all those years ago. That people, situations, change. We move on.'

'You're still lacking in specifics,' Alex stated dryly, and Shea's lips tightened irritatedly.

'Then just how specific do you want me to be?' She held his gaze. 'I'm afraid I'm not looking for any involvement, either emotional or physical. Is that specific enough for you?'

'Meaning there's someone else?' Alex demanded, and Shea raised her eyebrows in mock surprise.

'Does that have anything to do with it?'

Alex shrugged. 'It might explain a few things.'

'Perhaps there is someone else,' Shea shot back quickly. 'It's four years since Jamie's death. Would it be so strange?'

He rested his elbows on the arms of his chair, long fingers steepled, and his guarded gaze continued to bore into hers. 'No. I suppose not.'

The air in the room seemed to crackle with unbridled tension. Shea's heart thudded so loudly in her ears she knew he must hear it.

'Who is it?' he asked with studied indifference.

CHAPTER NINE

'I REALLY don't think that's any of your business,' she replied evenly, directly challenging his right to ask that question.

'Is it Aston? That wimp of a guy who's supposedly handling your affairs? He's a bit of a namby-pamby, isn't he? I almost signed the lease just to get rid of him.'

'David is a very nice young man.' She could almost cringe at the insipidness of her retort. But then, she acknowledged, she had admitted to herself that David Aston was not the most exciting person in the world.

'Nice?' Alex's lips twisted disdainfully. 'He could never handle you, Shea.'

Hot colour flooded over her at the implication behind his words and her throat tightened. 'I don't know what you mean.'

'Of course you do.'

Their eyes held, warred stormily, touched on sensuous memories they had in common, memories that held them immobile in the emotion-charged atmosphere around them.

'And we both know that I can. And have.' Alex's low voice drained the last vestige of strength from Shea's resistance.

Her contention had been shaky at best but now it was almost non-existent. Had he stood up right then, walked around her desk and taken her in his arms she knew she would have dissolved against him, would have clutched him to her, kissed him with a reckless abandonment so intense it frightened her. And disgusted her.

She made herself cling to that self-derision like a drowning man to a life preserver, using it to forcibly incite her previous anger toward him. At that particular moment it was her only protection.

How dare he suggest she had been so gullibly susceptible to his attraction? she goaded herself.

'Why, you arrogant—'

'But honest,' he interjected, and Shea stood up, grateful for her escalating ire.

Then the small knowing smile on his handsome face genuinely rekindled her anger towards him, and brought back all the pain, the hurt, his perfidy. Now, absolutely revitalised, her fury needed no goading. It unleashed like a coiled snake wanting to strike out at him, wound him as she'd been wounded.

'Perhaps I should put my cards on the table, Alex,' she bit out through thinned lips.

'By all means,' he said almost casually, and Shea drew a steadying breath.

She knew she was teetering on the very edge of control and if she fell over into irrationality who knew what she might scream at him in the agony of the moment? She had too much to lose.

'I've tried being polite but obviously you don't understand that,' she continued evenly. 'I'll concede that eleven years ago I was young and perhaps more foolish than most. I thought I was in love with you and my biggest mistake was that I thought you loved me, too. So naïve, wasn't I, Alex?' Her lips twisted in a humourless smile. 'Well, we all make mistakes. And if we're sensible we learn by them. We pick ourselves up, repair the damage and again if we're sensible we don't repeat the same mistake.' Shea paused and lifted her chin. 'I consider myself to be a very sensible person these days, Alex.'

He stared at her in silent scrutiny, a frown running two small furrows between his eyebrows and, clutching at her dignity, Shea subsided disdainfully onto her chair.

'Have I missed something here?' he asked then, his strong hand arcing in the direction of his broad chest. 'I'm the guilty party?'

'I don't think—' Shea began, but he continued as though she hadn't spoken.

'As I see it, you were the one who got married before the sound of my plane had faded into the distance.' He was sitting forward in his chair now, dark eyes boring into hers.

Shea reached for her pile of invoices, straightened them by tapping them on the desktop. 'I'm really far too busy to discuss this with you any further—'

'Well, I'm not,' Alex snapped and got abruptly to his feet. 'Let's drag it out into the open. It's been festering there between us since I came home.'

'This is ridiculous, Alex. And I don't see any point in raking it all over now.'

'I'm sure you don't,' he retorted sarcastically. 'So. Didn't you marry the first man who came along after I left?'

Shea's chair bumped the wall as she stood to face him. 'Left is the operative word. You *had* left, Alex,' she threw at him.

'And barely a month later you married Jamie. My own cousin,' he said, enunciating each word with heavy contempt.

'Jamie loved me and—'

'Do you think I didn't know that? Believe me, I knew. I always knew how he felt about you.' He strode across the small room to the window that looked out on the alley behind the shop, then turned back towards the desk. 'I used to spend most of the time wavering between pure exultation that you loved me more than you loved Jamie and a harrowing guilt that you did.'

And the tragedy, Shea thought with no little contrition, was that as a person Jamie was worth more than both of them. That knowledge was something she would have to live with forever. But she certainly didn't want to discuss it with Alex of all people.

'Well, it's all in the past now,' she made herself say evenly. 'Let's just leave it at that. Jamie and I had a good marriage and—'

Alex was across the room and around her desk in a couple of strides. He grasped her arm, his fingers biting into her flesh. 'And I don't suppose you knew or even cared that I knew, too, did you?'

'Let me go, Alex. You're hurting me.' Shea tried to free herself from his hold. 'I don't know what you're talking about.'

'Jamie told me how happy you were.' Alex gave a bitter laugh. 'And I died a thousand deaths over the years thinking of you with him. And then hating myself because I envied him so much it burned in my gut like an invidious fire that made me want to come back and break him with my bare hands. And he was just like a brother to me.'

He shook his head and his fingers released some of the pressure on her arm. His brown eyes were dark chocolate now, heavy with more than anger, and his gaze held hers enmeshed. 'I used to torture myself imagining you together, you kissing Jamie the way you used to kiss me, making love with him. And wondering if you remembered.' His eyes settled on her lips and wild heat washed over her. 'Did you, Shea?'

'Did I what?'

His thumb rubbed gently at the soft skin of her inner arm, brushing so close to the side of her breast. 'When you were making love with Jamie, did you ever imagine it was me?'

Shea's mouth was dry. Her whole body wanted to move towards him but with steely control she held herself rigidly apart. 'You dare to ask me that? You have no right—'

'Well, did you?' He shook her arm. 'Did you ever think about us? About how good we were together? And did you think of me?'

Shea swallowed as the reckless thunder of her heartbeats rose in her breast. In all honesty he'd never been that far from her thoughts. But she had no intention of admitting that to him. Now or ever.

'No, Alex. I rarely thought of you.' Her voice sounded reasonably steady and she drew some strength from that. 'I put all my memories of you in a tiny box and stowed it away in the fartherest, darkest corner of my mind. So no, Alex. I'm sorry if it wounds your manly pride, but I didn't think of you.'

'So you wiped me from your mind?' His narrowed gaze still held hers and then he gave a brief smile that didn't reach his eyes. 'I don't think so, Shea. I'm afraid I don't believe you. That's why you won't let me get too close now, isn't it? You're terrified because you know that I hold the key to that tiny box of yours. I'm the one who can unlock it, lift the lid on that cool composure you hold so dear. Isn't that the truth, Shea? I can give it back to you. Life with a capital L. Make you feel again that same aching desire we always had.'

'No.'

'Yes,' he said softly, the word flowing over her like warm oil on her heated skin. 'I know yes.'

The timbre of his voice, the clean male muskiness of him, assaulted her senses, waged a one-sided war on her self-control and she knew she was rapidly losing ground. Her stomach shivered with nervous desperation, yet began to grow warm with something far more potently dangerous.

She had to do something before she crumbled, before her hard-won resolve shattered right before his very eyes.

'Then why did you go?' Shea blurted before she could stop herself, and Alex closed his eyes for a moment, taking a deep breath.

'I explained why I was leaving. I wanted to get the best education, make something of myself.'

'Oh, yes. All I, me, myself. Alex had to have what Alex wanted, didn't he?'

'I admit I wanted you,' Alex said softly, and Shea gave a bitter laugh.

'As I said, Alex had to have what Alex wanted. Well, you had me, Alex. Although I'm not vain enough to think that you remember all that much about that now. Back then when it suited you, you conveniently forgot.'

'Forgot what?'

Shea bit off an uncharacteristic, unladylike oath.

'Forgot that we made love?' Alex's voice had dropped to the low inciting timbre Shea remembered so well.

And her vividly provocative recollections set her traitorous senses into a frenzy of rising desire. Her body craved the passion she knew he could awaken, that only he could satisfy.

'Forgot that I was your first lover?' Alex was continuing softly, sensually. 'That it was the most incredible experience of my life? And that it kept on being just as incredible?'

The air between them thickened again, expanded about them, and with each passing second it enveloped them even further into its oppressive web of sensual wanting.

'It *was* incredible, wasn't it, Shea? We made love because it was inevitable that we did. We were two halves of one whole. We dovetailed. And all the pieces fit so perfectly.'

'You're being disgusting,' Shea got out through her almost immobilised vocal chords.

'Disgusting? How so? Because I'm simply proving to you that I haven't forgotten? Because, believe me, I haven't. Not one moment of the times we were together. I could take you to each place.' His voice dropped even lower. 'I could point out the exact spot where we lay together. And tell you exactly how you felt in my arms. The smoothness of your skin in the moonlight. Every curve, every secret erotic place. And every sound you made when I touched you there—'

'Alex! Stop! Please.'

'Perhaps you're the one who's forgotten, Shea.'

Her head went up, her cheeks still touched by the flush that deepened the colour in her cheeks at his audacious words. Forgotten? She had tried so desperately to erase all memory of that time from her mind. But then late at night the dream would return to remind her.

Her eyes met his, held his gaze, and he couldn't help but read the truth in their green depths.

The corners of Alex's mouth rose faintly in a knowing smile. 'No.' The word held a blatant note of triumph. 'You haven't forgotten any more than I have. I knew that last night on the balcony,' he said softly as his hands reached for her.

'And when you were with Patti did you think of me?' she demanded levelly and she felt his whole body pause, each hard muscle tensed.

An omnipresent stillness fell between them as her words seemed to shriek so loudly it was deafening. Electricity sparked the air, made crazy patterns before Shea's eyes, and then, just as she thought she could bear the silence no longer he suddenly released her arm, turning from her to run a distracted hand through his hair.

'Did I think of you when I was with Patti? Constantly,' he said hoarsely. 'God help me. You never left my mind.'

'I don't want to hear this, Alex.'

'No?' He swung back to face her. 'Why not? You're the one who asked the sixty-four-thousand-dollar question and now you want to run from the answer. Yes, when I made love to my wife I thought of you.'

Shea shook her head but he took a step closer until he was mere millimetres from her.

'Does it make you squeamish, Shea?' he asked brutally. 'I know it does me. To know that when I touched another woman I always dreamed I was touching you, always wished it was you. Does that answer your question? So if you want to know if I suffered for leaving you then the answer's yes. A thousand times, yes.'

Shea could only gaze up at him, her mind in a turmoil.

'And the cruelest part of it,' he added derisively, 'was that I never loved Patti. And she knew that.'

'Then why did you marry her?' Shea asked him thickly.

'Because I'd lost you.' He shook his head slightly. 'No. Because I felt you'd betrayed me.'

'I betrayed you?' Shea repeated incredulously. 'You have a short memory, Alex.'

'Longer than yours, apparently. But that's beside the point. As you so rightly said, all that's in the past. It's the present we should be worrying about.' He paused slightly. 'I think we have a future, Shea.'

'A future?' Shea shook her head. 'Oh, no, Alex. You're wrong there. I don't intend to rake over old embers trying to breathe fire into the ashes.'

'I'd say the flames never died. They're still burning. They wouldn't need any banking.' He reached out and ran his finger down the line of her jaw, let his fingertip touch lightly on her lips, and Shea drew back as though she'd been shot.

'Don't touch me, Alex, or—'

'Why fight it or me, Shea. You know we strike sparks off each other. We always have.'

'No!'

'No?' He raised one fine eyebrow. 'Then prove me wrong.'

His lips came down and claimed hers for long exciting moments before he raised his head, his eyes telling her *I told you so*.

Shea pulled away. 'All right, Alex. I'd be the first to admit you do have a winning technique. But before you claim your victory let me tell you it's a hollow one. I've been alone for four years so I suppose I'd be considered fair and reasonable game. What conquest's that?'

'Since when has it ever been a war between us?' Alex put in ironically, but Shea continued as though he hadn't spoken.

'But that's immaterial. I don't intend to be anyone's prize.' Shea gave an almost imperceptible shrug. 'I was too close to you, Alex. I built my life on you. And I was pretty devastated when you left. Quite frankly, I don't ever again want to feel that way about any man.'

Alex went to comment but Shea held up her hand. 'But, most of all, I don't want to get involved with you or anyone at this stage in my life. I have my son to raise and my business is expanding so I have little free time. So, you see, Alex. I don't need what you're offering.'

'And exactly what is it that you think I'm offering?' Alex said lightly.

'On present evidence and at the risk of sounding staid and old-fashioned, an affair, of the purely physical kind. Fun, at least for you, while it lasts, but over when you leave again.'

'Fun only for me?' he repeated sardonically. 'It would be mutual, I promise.'

'Thanks, but no thanks, Alex.'

The corners of his mouth quirked momentarily. 'And you think I want to have some sort of clandestine affair? Clandestine?' He gave a soft laugh. 'It sounds almost proper.'

'And I'm sure what you have in mind is far from that. Well, I don't intend to sneak away at the dead of night like I used to, to join you in some sordid tryst. I'm twenty-eight years old, for heaven's sake. These days I prefer the comfort of a bed.'

'Comfort is fine by me,' Alex said with mock seriousness. 'Would it matter if it was your bed or mine?'

'Alex, I'm not going to sleep with you,' Shea stated exasperatedly.

A slight noise made them both turn sharply towards the door to see David Aston paused halfway into the room. His face was flushed and Shea realised he must surely have heard what she had said. Her own blush rose to reach the roots of her hair.

David gave a discreet cough. 'My apologies, Shea. Debbie seems to be busy with a customer and so I thought I'd come right in. That is, I didn't realise you weren't alone. We, ah, I told your mother-in-law I'd call. At ten.' He swallowed and glanced at his wristwatch. 'I'll wait outside, shall I?'

'No.' Shea spoke quickly. 'Come in, David. Alex was just leaving.'

'We were getting around to discussing the lease,' Alex reminded her easily. 'I've checked out the contract.'

'I'm sure you have,' she replied, matching his tone. 'David's assured you it's fairly standard. Haven't you, David?'

'Oh, of course. You can be quite sure of that, Shea.' David stepped into the room and set his briefcase on the desk, turning to address Alex. 'It's all above board. My firm is a respected member of the—'

Alex waved him to silence. 'We need to talk about the terms, Shea.' Alex's brown eyes held Shea's gaze and she felt another flush of embarrassment wash her cheeks.

Alex was humiliating David and David was allowing him to do it. She felt a surge of irritation with both of them.

'If you want more money, Alex, you can discuss it with David.'

The other man's glance slid from Shea to Alex and he coughed nervously again. 'Shea, I really think the terms are quite generous,' he began, and then saw the sudden hardening of her expression. 'But of course, I'd be quite prepared to negotiate on your behalf. Do you have a preferable time?' he asked Alex.

Alex held Shea's gaze for long moments before he moved. 'I'll let you know,' he said evenly, and Shea made herself smile dismissively as she held out her hand. 'Fine. Then I'll see you later, Alex.'

He took long seconds to take her hand and he held it far longer than was necessary. His hard stare also told her their conversation was far from finished. 'Be assured you shall,' he said softly before giving David a curt nod as he left them.

Shea slowly released the breath she hadn't been aware she was holding. And she reluctantly turned to face David's obvious disapproval. That she had made a bad business move by suggesting more money kept him waffling on for what seemed like hours and by the time he, too, eventually left she had a throbbing headache.

And she spent the whole of the evening half listening for the sound of a car turning into the driveway that would herald Alex's arrival. But he didn't come.

*   *   *

'Thank heavens, you're here.' Debbie met Shea as she walked wearily into the shop the next afternoon.

'Is there no rest for the wicked?' she asked with a wry grin. The round of visiting distributors had seemed endless today and now it appeared her day wasn't yet over. 'What's the problem?'

'Sue Gavin rang,' Debbie told her, and Shea set her briefcase down, her muscles suddenly weak.

'Is Niall all right?' she asked quickly, and Debbie nodded.

'It's not Niall. Your mother-in-law's been taken ill. Sue said they'd rushed her to hospital.'

Fear clutched at Shea again. 'Norah? When was this?'

Debbie looked at her watch. 'About half an hour ago I'd say. I've been ringing around the distributors trying to catch you.'

'Did Sue say what was wrong? How serious it was?'

Debbie shook her head. 'No. Just that they'd rushed Mrs Finlay to hospital by ambulance.'

'All right.' Shea took a deep steadying breath. 'I'll go straight up to the hospital but I'll have to leave you to close again.'

'Oh, that's no trouble.' Debbie assured her quickly. 'I just hope Mrs Finlay's all right.'

Shea hurried back out to her car and drove the short distance to the hospital as quickly as she could. She then spent interminable minutes at the reception desk while the young woman found out where Norah was. Shea then followed her directions along the corridor to the room number she'd been given.

As she approached, a nurse came out of the room and Shea saw with no little relief that it was a young woman she knew by sight.

'Oh, hello, Shea,' the young woman said brightly enough. 'I guess you're here to see your mother-in-law. We're just preparing her for surgery.'

'Surgery?' Shea frowned worriedly and the nurse patted her arm.

'We do gall bladders all the time. Give us five minutes and then you can go in for a few minutes if you like, although she'll probably be getting a little groggy. I'll come and get you when we've finished. OK?'

Shea thanked her and hurried over to the pay phone on the wall, dialling her neighbour's number with shaking fingers.

'Sue? It's Shea. I'm at the hospital.'

'Thank heavens. How's Norah?'

'About to go in for surgery on her gall bladder. I'm going to see her in a few minutes. What happened?'

'I was in the back yard and she called out to me. She said she was having another gall bladder attack and she just crumpled up onto the grass. I raced over and rang her doctor. He came and then called for the ambulance. I wanted to find someone to look after the twins and go with her but she wouldn't let me. She just said to call you.'

Shea groaned softly. 'Thanks, Sue, for helping Norah out. Do you think you could keep Niall over with you when he gets home from soccer practice? I want to stay here with Norah.'

'Sure. Don't worry about Niall. Give Norah my love and we'll see you when we see you.'

Shea hung up and nervously paced the hallway waiting for the nurse to reappear. However, before she did, Norah's doctor joined her.

'Ah, Shea. I'm glad you're here. We're going to take Norah into surgery and do something about her gall stones.'

'Is she—? I mean—?' Shea swallowed. 'Will she be all right?'

The doctor pursed his lips. 'Well, I've been wanting her to have the surgery for months but now the decision's been taken out of her hands. As you can imagine I'd have preferred it not to have happened this way but—' He shrugged. 'She's in good shape otherwise so barring complications she should be fine.'

'The nurse said I could see her before she goes in.'

At that moment the same nurse came out of Norah's room and Shea went in with the doctor. Her mother-in-law was tucked neatly into a mobile bed. Her eyes were closed and she looked small and fragile and Shea's heart sank. She hurried across to her and clasped her hand.

Norah's eyes fluttered open. 'Shea. Have I had my op yet?'

The doctor took over, checking Norah, quietly reassuring her, and then he left them alone.

'Oh, my dear. I'm just so glad you arrived before I went in,' Norah said, a little more awake now.

'I can only stay a few minutes before you go down to the theatre.'

'I'm glad you're here.' Norah's fingers tightened and Shea gave her mother-in-law's hand a squeeze back. 'I want to talk to you.'

'Don't try to talk,' Shea said softly. 'Just relax and let the medication take over.'

'No, Shea. I must talk to you.' Norah struggled to sit up and Shea soothed her back onto the bed.

'We can talk after the operation. They're much quicker now. And the doctor tells me they have a far more simple way of removing the gall stones these days. You'll be back before you know it.'

'No. I've wanted to talk to you about this for so long. But I was afraid.'

'Norah—'

'I know the truth, love. I always have known.'

'The truth?' Shea repeated softly, and Norah again clutched at Shea's hand.

'About Niall. I know Jamie couldn't be his father. You have to tell Alex, Shea. He has a right to know.'

Norah's eyelids fluttered as Shea stood there, her whole body icy cold. Norah knew? But how?

Norah opened her eyes again. 'Niall's Alex's son, isn't he?'

'But, Norah, how—?' Shea's frozen lips moved stiffly. 'Jamie said we wouldn't tell anyone.'

Her mother-in-law moved her hand negatingly. 'Jamie didn't have to tell me, love. And it never ever mattered to me. Niall's a beautiful child and Alex should know he has a fine son.' She closed her eyes again and this time Shea could see she was asleep.

She stood and held Norah's hand and it was as though time simply stood still.

How could Norah have known if Jamie hadn't told her? She knew Niall looked so much like Alex but he had her colouring, too. He was much fairer than Alex. Jamie and Alex both had the Finlay family features. They could have passed for brothers.

Yet how could Norah have known? Jamie had given her his word he'd never tell anyone. How had Norah guessed? Shea looked down at her mother-in-law, wanting to ask her, but Norah was fast asleep.

The nurse returned and spoke cheerfully to Shea as she wheeled Norah away on her mobile hospital bed but Shea could barely take in the other woman's assurances. She just stood numbly in the hospital hallway and watched the little procession move away.

She swallowed the lump in her throat. She had learned to love Norah as much as she would have loved her own mother. Yet now, with Norah's revelations, would their safe and secure little world ever be the same? Knowing that Norah knew about Niall completely changed the focus of their relationship.

As Norah and the nurse moved around the corner and out of sight Shea turned away only to realise she was not alone in the corridor.

Alex stood in front of her. His face was slightly pale and he was looking at her as though he hadn't seen her before.

With a super-human effort she pulled herself together and dashed a tear from her damp cheek. 'Oh, Alex. You've missed seeing Norah. They've just wheeled her away. It's her gall bladder. But the doctor says he's sure she should be fine.'

Her words died away as his harsh expression penetrated her shock.

'Alex?' she said faintly, questioningly. And then she turned cold as the thought crossed her mind that perhaps he'd overheard her conversation with Norah. No. How could he have? They'd been alone in the room, Norah and herself.

She glanced up at him again. Dear Lord! He couldn't have heard Norah.

'They have to operate immediately,' Shea repeated, needing to fill the pressing silence. 'She's had trouble with her gall bladder for years but she didn't want to have the surgery. The doctor says now it's a case of having to have it.'

She stopped and slid a nervous glance at him. His face seemed to have a little more colour now and she tried to tell herself he was simply anxious about Norah. He would be, she assured herself.

'The doctor also said,' Shea continued, 'that Norah should cope with the operation quite well. She has no other medical problems that could cause concern. She'll be fine, Alex. I'm sure she will. We just have to wait it out.'

Alex still stood there silently and Shea went to put a reassuring hand on his arm but he drew back as though she had been about to do him some injury.

Her heartbeats skipped apprehensively. 'Alex?' Her voice sounded thin and high and she swallowed quickly. 'Alex, what is it?' she asked breathily as a tiny voice inside her screamed at her that he knew her secret, that he knew about Niall.

'Let's go.' He moved then, reaching out, fingers taking firm hold of her arm as he turned her, started them walking swiftly back along the corridor.

'Alex, what—?'

'Not here, Shea. We need some privacy.' He thrust open the door of the first waiting room and when he'd ascertained it was empty he pushed her inside, closing the door behind him with an ominous click. He leaned back against the door, hand still holding the doorknob, and they stared at each other across the couple of metres that separated them.

Shea made herself hold his gaze, trying to convince herself he hadn't overheard Norah's entreaties, telling herself that if by some dreadful misfortune he had then she had to brazen this out. Her son was her world and therefore her whole world was at stake. But before she could begin some defence, he spoke.

'How could you do that?' he asked, his voice hoarse and thick and she flinched as a shaft of pain rose to swell in her chest.

Panic rose with the pain and she fought desperately to hold on to her control. She couldn't let go. 'Do what?' she got out. 'Alex, I don't know what you're talking about.'

She glanced about her, seeking something. A seat she could sink into, another door through which she could make her escape. 'And whatever it is, I think you should wait until after Norah—' Her voice faded on her as he moved, came towards her.

In two lithe strides he was within inches of her and the angry fire in his eyes held her motionless.

'You were carrying my son and you didn't tell me about it?' he demanded through clenched teeth.

'Alex, this is ridiculous. I can explain—'

'Explain!' The word was like a rapier thrust. 'This I have to hear.'

'I take it you overheard Norah. She'd been sedated. She didn't know what she was saying. I'm sure I don't know why she—'

'No more lies, Shea.' Alex held up his hand. 'Norah spoke the truth. I can see it in your eyes so cut the prevarication and just answer my question. Why didn't you tell me you were carrying my child?'

Shea felt as though her racing heartbeats were going to choke her and she swallowed convulsively. 'You forget, Alex. You'd decided we were going to cool it for a while. You were going away to do your own thing. For a few years or so. I couldn't wait that long. What was I supposed to tell you?'

'How about the truth. My God! Do you think I'd have left you behind if I'd known?'

Shea shrugged. 'We'll never know, will we? But I think it all worked out for the best.'

'The best? The best for whom?'

'For us all.'

'All meaning you and Jamie? Or just you?'

'No. I mean it solved all our problems. You got to do what you wanted to do without being made to feel you had some obligation to me.' Shea swallowed again. 'I had a father for my child and Jamie, well, Jamie loved me and I—' She shrugged.

'Do you know how sick to the back teeth I am of hearing that? About how much Jamie loved you?' Alex ran a shaking hand through his hair and took a deep breath. 'And now you want to ensure I continue to suffer by telling me you let him raise my son.'

'No one could have done a better job than Jamie did.'

'Do you think I don't know that? Do you think that makes it any easier to bear?' He regarded her with burning intensity. 'Do you know, thinking about you and Jamie together, well, I thought that was the most pain I'd have to bear. But I was wrong.'

'Alex, please. Don't—' Shea shook her head and turned away from him, putting some space between them. Tears welled in her eyes but she fought them back and drew herself together. Slowly she moved back to face him.

'I know you want to,' Shea swallowed, forcing some semblance of calmness into her voice. 'I know you want to discuss this, Alex, and I will. But not now. After Norah's operation. Can we leave it until then?'

Alex ran his hand along the line of his jaw. He showed no sign that he needed a shave but the faint rasp of his day-old beard echoed in the small room.

Shea nervously tucked a loose tendril of hair back behind her ear. 'I can understand that you'd want to know—'

'That's big of you, Shea,' he interrupted sarcastically.

'But this couldn't be a worse time. We're both upset about Norah and—'

'Norah wanted us to discuss it, if you recall,' Alex bit out angrily.

'Please, Alex. I need time. I never—'

'You were never going to tell me, were you, Shea?' he asked flatly, and she looked away from the pain in his eyes.

'I—' Shea shook her head slightly. 'I honestly don't know,' she said softly.

Alex strode across the room, stood with his back to her, one strong hand rubbing absently at the tight muscles in the back of his neck. Then he swung back towards her, his face set.

'Well, there's one thing *I* know, Shea. I want my son.'

CHAPTER TEN

'WHAT... What do you mean?'

'I mean I've missed the first ten years of his life. I don't intend to miss any more.'

'You'd try to take Niall from me? Alex, you wouldn't.' Shea lifted her chin. 'I won't let you. You couldn't. Anyway, no court in the land would allow that. I'll—'

'You think that of me? That I'd use the courts to try to take Niall away from you?' Alex swore under his breath.

'Well, you said—'

'I meant I want to get to know Niall,' he said concisely. 'I want to be involved in his life. I want to contribute to his upbringing.'

'I can provide for Niall. He's never wanted for anything. I'm not exactly a pauper. My business is doing well—'

'Money has nothing to do with it.'

'Then what did you mean?'

'I just want to be part of his life.' He held out his hands and let them fall in exasperation. 'Is that so hard to believe, Shea?'

She looked up at him and their gazes were locked together. Shea's was the first to fall. Her whole body felt numb and she wondered if she was suffering some form of shock. Whatever it was, she knew she was close to breaking point. Her worst nightmare had become reality.

'I can't take much more of this right now, Alex. Could

we please leave it until,' Shea swallowed, 'at least until after Norah's operation?'

'We've already left it for eleven years,' he said flatly, and Shea rubbed her hand over her eyes.

'This is just too much emotion for me to handle at the moment.' She looked up at him again. 'Would another few hours hurt?'

'I suppose not,' he eventually agreed with obvious reluctance. 'This isn't the best time to have this conversation, I'll admit. But when would be?'

He strode across to stand in front of the only decoration in the room, a tastefully-framed, pastel-shaded painting of a spray of flowers that was hanging on the opposite wall. But Shea knew he wasn't seeing it.

She watched him warily, and she realised that even in this long-dreaded moment of confrontation, part of her was still traitorously attracted to him, her eyes almost subconsciously taking in his appearance.

His slacks were dark grey and he'd apparently discarded his suit jacket before he'd entered the hospital. He'd also removed his tie and the sleeves of his shirt were folded back almost to his elbows.

'I never for one moment suspected that Niall was my son. Jamie told me you'd had a bad time, that he was premature. And I believed him.' He turned to look at her again. 'I've lost ten years of my son's life.'

'Alex, please—'

He said something under his breath and turned away again. 'You're right. This isn't the time. I can't possibly be rational about this now. If I ever can be.'

'As I said before, I did what I thought was best at the time,' Shea found herself saying and then broke off, knowing she had taken the defensive. 'I can't change that.'

'Ain't that the truth,' he said with feeling and then he sighed. 'I don't remember Norah having problems with her gall bladder,' he said then, his broad back still to her.

His change of subject disconcerted Shea almost as much as the sight of his strong shoulders moulded by the thin silk shirt seemed to be doing, and she moistened her suddenly dry lips.

'She's been getting the pain every so often for some years,' she got out disjointedly as she valiantly pulled herself together. 'The doctor told her she'd have to have the operation eventually but she kept postponing it. Dr Robbins had her booked in for a couple of months' time but it seems the situation was taken out of her hands and they had to operate today.'

A lump rose in Shea's throat but she swallowed and gave a slight cough. 'When I spoke to the doctor earlier he said she'd be fine but—' Shea bit her lip. 'I can't help worrying. Norah's not young any more and—'

Alex had turned back to face her.

'I just can't,' Shea swallowed again, 'I can't imagine life without her, that's all. She's always been there for me and for Niall.'

At that moment the door opened and the same nurse stuck her head into the room. 'So this is where you are, Shea.' She came inside and then did a double take when she noticed Alex as he moved across to join Shea. 'Well, for heaven's sake. Alex Finlay.' She smiled brightly. 'I heard you were back in Byron.'

There were certain drawbacks involved in attending a reasonably small school, Shea decided. Everyone knew everyone else. She'd forgotten the nurse would remember Alex, too. Didn't everybody? she asked herself a little caustically.

'How's Norah?' she asked quickly, and the nurse turned back to her, with noticeable reluctance, Shea reflected uncharitably.

'She's out of the theatre and we've got her in recovery. The operation went very well but she won't be coherent for a few hours.' She glanced at her fob watch. 'Why don't you go on home and have some dinner and come back about seven-thirty?'

'Are you sure she's all right?' Shea persisted, and the nurse smiled and shook her head in mock exasperation.

'Of course she is. Now stop worrying, Shea. Come on.' She held the door open for them. 'You can pop in and see her if you like even though she won't know you're there. Then you can get Alex to take you home.'

'I have my own car,' Shea told them as they walked down the corridor but neither the nurse nor Alex commented on her independent stand.

They tip-toed into Norah's room but, as the nurse had said she would be, the older woman was fast asleep. Shea's heart contracted. She squeezed Norah's hand, almost overwhelmed with the need to tell her how much she had appreciated Norah giving her a home, loving her like a daughter, being such a support after Jamie's death. Tears welled in her eyes and one trickled down her cheek. And she knew she wasn't just crying for Norah.

The nurse passed her a tissue and made soft, reassuring noises. 'Go on home now, Shea,' she said quietly. 'I'll see you later if you get back before my shift ends.'

They filed back out of the room and the nurse turned to Alex. 'Good to see you home again, Alex. Have to catch up with you some time and hear all about your adventures overseas.'

Alex smiled and said something non-committal as he took Shea's arm, leading her along the hallway and out into the parking lot.

'I'll drive you home,' he stated as they squinted into the setting sun. 'We'll leave your car here and collect it tonight.'

'Don't be silly, Alex. I'm quite capable of driving myself home,' Shea began, but he kept his hold on her and started her in the direction of the maroon Jaguar.

Shea stopped and firmly loosened his grip on her arm. 'Must you always be so overbearing? I told you I can drive myself home.'

His brown eyes burned into hers for one heavy moment and then he sighed loudly. 'And must you always be so argumentative? Is there any chance you might simply go with the flow for a change?' he suggested drily, and then at the stubborn look on her face he made an acquiescing movement with his hands. 'So. This blue one's yours, isn't it? Where are your car keys?'

Shea took them out of her pocket as he held out his hand for them. In a completely reflex action she passed them to him and he unlocked the passenger side door of her car before turning back to her.

'We'll leave the Jag here and you can drive me home then,' he said easily as he passed the keys back to her.

Shea stood there holding the bunch of keys, watching as he lowered himself into her small car. She opened her mouth to protest but before she could form any words he glanced up at her.

'Niall will be waiting to hear how his grandmother is.'

His comment made her jaw tense on what she wanted to say to him. Instead she turned on her heel and walked around to the driver's side, sliding in behind the wheel. Niall would be worried, she knew. Trust Alex to remind her. He knew, had always known, just how to press the right buttons.

The engine faltered and then fired and Shea drove out of the car park without making any attempt at conversation. Alex was silent, too, and she was relieved about that. She felt a surge of hysteria rise inside her and she fought to quell it, unsure whether her reaction would be to scream at him or weep uncontrollably.

If only she wasn't so uncertain of Alex's intentions towards Niall. He'd said he wanted to get to know his son, be part of his life. But to do that he'd have to be part of her life, as well, and Shea wasn't sure she could cope with that. As it stood she'd have to go along with him until they could come to some resolution.

How she wished she could be alone with her thoughts, to try to sort out the jumble of numbing impressions that seemed to be ricocheting about inside her head, making her feel tense and on edge.

To learn that Norah knew the truth about Niall, and about the subterfuge she and Jamie had concocted to cover that truth was bad enough. But for Alex to have found out about Niall as well—

Shea's stomach twisted into knots again, making her feel physically ill. She swallowed, fought to calm her quivering nerves. This was not the time to go to pieces. She had to keep her wits about her so she could protect her son.

She slid a sideways glance at Alex. She was fairly sure he wouldn't tell Niall, but just in case she would have to see she didn't give Alex the opportunity. That meant keeping some emotional distance between Alex, and Niall and herself. It would be no mean feat, knowing Alex's strength of purpose. However, no matter what it took she would do it. Niall was not going to be the casualty in this battle between his mother and his natural father.

Shea tried to formulate a plan in her mind. Her first objective was to see that Alex didn't have any contact with Niall until she had sorted out in her mind the best way to handle the situation. All her instincts shied away from telling Niall that Alex was his father but she knew if he was to hear the truth from anyone it should come from her.

She pulled to a halt for a red light. Alex sat beside her, apparently completely relaxed, one arm lying comfortably along the window ledge. But her gaze was drawn to his strong tanned hand resting lightly on his thigh. His arm, where it showed beneath the folded-back cuff of his shirt, was covered in fine fairish hair that shone in the orange light from the setting sun, a perfect foil for his obviously expensive gold watch.

She noticed a small pale scar on top of his hand above his thumb, the result, she knew, of a mishap with a knife when he was cleaning some fish he and Jamie had caught.

Shea could remember that incident so vividly it was incredible to think it had happened all of fifteen years ago. She remembered she'd felt faint as the bright red blood ran from the wound.

Somehow she'd grabbed a tea towel and staunched the flow while Jamie raced off in search of his mother. By the time Norah arrived the bleeding had stopped and the wound had only needed to be covered.

Yet the small scar remained, a testament to the days when Alex had been the centre of her universe. Tears welled in her eyes and she wanted to reach out, run her finger over that thin white line, draw back those carefree days of love and laughter. Before the pain began.

But of course she remained unmoving in her seat. And she steeled herself against the weakening effect his nearness always seemed to have on her these days, regardless of the aversion she had for him.

It was so imperative that she ensure Alex kept his distance. Any mother wanted to protect her child and now she had to shield Niall from what had always been her worst nightmare.

'Alex?' she said quickly. 'Don't tell Niall. Please. Not yet.'

'You think I'd do that?' he asked incredulously and turned away from her.

Shea swallowed, realising the traffic lights had turned to green and she accelerated smoothly through the intersection wishing she had agreed to let Alex drive her home. Then perhaps when Alex dropped her off she could have thanked him quickly and hurried inside before Niall was aware he was there.

However, that was not to be now and even as she turned the car into the driveway Niall jumped over the low fence between their place and the Gavins's.

'Mum! How's Gran?' he called out before Shea was even out of the car.

Shea plastered a smile on her face and gave him a reassuring hug. 'She's fine.'

Sue Gavin stood by the fence, one of her ten-month-old twins on her hip. 'Has Norah had the operation?' she asked, obviously keeping her tone light for Niall's sake, and Shea nodded.

'She's still in recovery but the nurse said she was doing well.'

'That's great,' Sue smiled, and Shea thanked her for looking after Niall.

'No trouble,' she said as her other twin began to cry inside the house. With a rueful wave she walked away to check on the problem.

'Can we go up and see Gran?' Niall asked anxiously as Sue left them.

'Of course we can. But after dinner. She'll be properly awake by then.'

Alex closed his door and it was a testament to Niall's concern for his grandmother that he hadn't noticed Alex until that moment.

'Alex! Hi!' He walked around the car to stop and look up at Alex with a grin that quickly faded. 'Did you know Gran's in the hospital?'

Alex nodded. 'Yes, I know.'

'But Mum says she's okay.' He turned back towards his mother. 'She *is* okay, isn't she, Mum? I mean, Gran isn't going to...' he paused and swallowed quickly. 'She isn't going to die like Dad did, is she?'

Shea felt a painful lump of unshed tears rise to choke her as she looked at her son's pale face but it was Alex who came to her rescue.

He reached out and rested his hand on Niall's shoulder. 'As you probably already know, your grandmother's had problems with her gall bladder,' he told Niall evenly. 'The doctors have new ways of doing this type of operation these days, far less traumatic for the patient. I'm pretty sure Gran will be out of hospital in a few days and then she'll just have to take things easy for a while.'

Niall's gaze solemnly held Alex's and then the young boy seemed to relax. 'That's good. I was, well, a bit worried. You know. After Dad.'

'That's understandable,' Alex agreed and straightened, his brown eyes meeting Shea's for a moment before his lashes fell to shield his expression.

'Have you been at the hospital with Mum?' Niall asked him, and when Alex replied that he had, Niall nodded slightly. 'I'm glad you were there, Alex. With Mum. I mean, it was good she wasn't on her own while Gran had her operation.'

'I'm glad it's all over,' Shea put in quickly. 'And hopefully, it will improve Gran's health.'

Niall gave a soft chuckle. 'Do you suppose now Gran will be able to eat those cream cakes she's always loved?'

He took hold of his mother's hand and ingenuously slipped his other hand into one of Alex's, glancing up at him. 'Gran used to love cream cakes before they started to play her up,' he told him, using one of Norah's expressions.

'I seem to recall they were her favourites,' Alex replied as Niall started them towards the house.

'Will you be staying for dinner, Alex?' he asked formally, and Alex gave a laugh.

'Sure will. Then we can all go up to the hospital together to see Gran.'

Shea unlocked the door, swallowing her impatience. Alex thought he had everything worked out. Innocently aided and abetted by Niall.

'I've just had a thought,' Alex stated with mock seriousness. 'Am I taking a chance staying for dinner, Niall? I mean, how's your mother's cooking? I have a feeling it wasn't so great in the old days.'

Niall laughed and made a so-so movement with his hand. 'It's fair to middling. But Gran's is better,' he added with a teasing look at his mother.

'Tread carefully, you two,' Shea said as lightly as she could. 'I'm sure you know that old saying, don't you? A cook in the hand is worth two in the bush.'

'I think we'd best be quiet, Alex.' Niall put his hand over his mouth, his eyes innocently wide.

'Mum's the word,' Alex added, and Niall laughed delightedly.

A shaft of pain shot through Shea. She swallowed as a crazy combination of emotions clutched at her, not the least her love for her son. And the knowledge that Alex now had the power to bring her world crashing down if he chose to do so.

'Have you got much homework?' Shea addressed Niall and her voice sounded a little sharp to her ears. He glanced at her and then shook his head.

'Pete and I did our homework together. I finished it while I was waiting for you to come home from the hospital.'

Shea realised guiltily that she was being unfair to Niall, taking out on her son her impatience with herself. 'Then maybe you should pop in and have a shower while I see to dinner,' she suggested a little more lightly.

'A shower? Oh, Mum!' Niall protested and then reluctantly sniffed his shirt and groaned. 'I guess I have been to soccer training so I suppose I'd better get cleaned up.' He wrinkled his nose. 'Otherwise they mightn't let me into see Gran, hey? I'll be really quick.'

He ran back down the hallway leaving Alex and Shea standing in the kitchen alone together.

Shea felt a wave of colour wash up over her face. She knew Alex was watching her and now that Niall had gone she perversely wanted him back.

'I'll see what I can find to eat,' she said hurriedly and opened the refrigerator.

On the second shelf was a crusty steak and kidney pie which Norah must have made before she was taken ill. Shea drew it out and tried to infuse a natural cheerfulness into her voice.

'You and Niall will be pleased to see this pie,' she remarked and slipped it into the oven. 'You won't have to take a chance on my cooking.'

Alex made no comment and when Shea turned he'd moved closer to her, was regarding her with a narrowed, intense gaze.

'Let me take care of you and Niall,' he said softly. 'Marry me, Shea.'

CHAPTER ELEVEN

'MARRY you?' Shea instinctively took a step away from him as her tight throat hoarsely repeated his words, unconsciously emphasising the second one.

'Why not?' Alex followed her, was so much closer now, and he reached up, his fingers trailing gently down the bare skin of her arm.

And Shea shivered in response. Her stomach muscles contracted and another flash of scrambled emotions zigzagged through her. Aversion, she told herself, but knew there was more than a little yearning anticipation.

'It would be the perfect solution.'

His detached justification tore through Shea and a coldness snatched at her heart. She drew herself together and moved aside from him, deliberately reaching for the broccoli, beginning to wash it under the tap.

'Perfect for whom?' she asked disdainfully. 'Perfect for you? Why would I need to ask that?' She gave a cool smile. 'Of course it would be perfect for you.'

'I meant I could be part of Niall's life. And yours,' he added quietly. His low-pitched tone played over her, so effortlessly evoking the familiar craving reaction of her traitorous senses.

'I believe I've already assured you I'm quite happy with my life the way it is, Alex.' As the words fell from her mouth she was busy berating her inner voice which loudly cried disbelief. 'And I don't feel any need to change that.'

'Not even if it's in Niall's best interests?'

Shea raised her head and met his gaze. 'Oh, no, Alex. Don't try to pull that on me. I won't bow to emotional blackmail.'

'I had and have no intention of doing that,' Alex put in.

'Does Niall look like he's suffered for not having you in his life?' she continued stormily and was momentarily taken aback when she saw a flash of pain in Alex's brown eyes before his lashes fell to shield his expression. Her barb had gone home but she felt no surge of elation at her success. Just an answering agony that caught her in the chest.

'No,' Alex agreed flatly and ran a tired hand across his jaw, the faint rasp of his day-old beard echoing in the charged air as it had in the hospital waiting room. 'You know I can't say that. Niall's a great kid.' He paused. 'But can you honestly say that my son's life would not be better from now on if it included me?'

Their eyes held, Alex's challenging, and Shea swallowed in anguish. She was valiantly trying to re-group her defences when Niall dashed into the room.

'Finished,' he said brightly, and Shea busied herself with the vegetables.

'That was quick,' she said banally, and Niall grinned.

'I know. And I didn't give myself a lick and a promise. Cross my heart. You can even check behind my ears. I hurried because I didn't want to miss talking to you, Alex.' He smiled up at the man and Shea glanced away from her son's face as she tried to deny the root of her feelings.

She refused to acknowledge that she could be jealous, envious of her son's adoration of Alex. Of his father, she reminded herself.

Niall had simply taken to Alex because he was so much like Jamie. And she knew how much he missed Jamie, the only father he'd known. Had she any right to deny her son the company of his biological father? she asked herself painfully.

Alex was suggesting he and Niall set the table and they moved about the kitchen chatting easily.

'My coach says he used to play rugby league with you before he saw the light,' Niall said and chuckled at Alex's expression. 'Before he took up soccer,' Niall explained. 'You know, the real footy game,' he teased lightly.

Alex laughed, too, the sound flowing over Shea in a conflicting wave of need and denial of that need. They continued to badger each other about the merits of each game as Shea busied herself putting the vegetables in the microwave and checking the pie in the oven.

Eventually the meal was on the table and they sat down, Niall not noticing that Alex and his mother rarely spoke to each other.

'I'm playing soccer tomorrow morning,' Niall said, his eyes on his plate. 'If you're not doing anything, Alex, maybe you could come and watch the game,' he added tentatively.

'Alex will probably be busy,' Shea began, wanting to protect her son from rejection.

'Oh.' Niall sighed. 'That's OK. I just thought that, well, you said you had to work this Saturday, Mum, because Debbie's going to be away, so you couldn't come. I thought Alex might be able to come instead.' He turned hopefully to Alex.

Alex's gaze met Shea's and then he smiled at his son. 'As it happens I do have a few hours to spare tomorrow and I'd like to come and watch you play.'

'You would?' Niall beamed. 'Hey, that's great! Pete's dad always comes and sometimes his mum. And Mum always comes when she can get away from the shop. Even Gran comes sometimes. But I guess she can't tomorrow.'

'What time does the game start?' Alex asked, and Niall eagerly filled him in as Shea began collecting and rinsing the dishes.

She wanted to warn her son not to get too involved with Alex, that getting too close to him was too dangerous, a pleasure that eventually meant pain. And then she tortured herself by speculating about who was the more likely to be injured by Alex. Niall or herself?

They arrived at the hospital by taxi after a small hitch when Shea's car chose that moment to refuse to start. She would ring the Automobile Club in the morning, she told Alex when he offered to fix it for her later that evening. As it stood Alex would have to drive them home from the hospital in his Jaguar and as they walked up the passageway to Norah's room Shea silently cursed all mechanical objects and their inconsistencies. Once again she was forced to take Alex's help.

Niall walked between his mother and Alex, solemnly carrying the bunch of flowers they'd chosen for his grandmother at the florist shop. His young face broke into a huge grin as they walked into the small ward to see Norah sitting back against her pillows.

'Gran!' He raced across the room and stopped just as suddenly at the bed. 'Can I hug you or is your operation too painful?'

'I think a gentle hug might be just what I need.' Norah smiled down at him.

'These are for you.' Niall proffered the flowers. 'There's some roses in there because we knew they were your favourites.'

Alex and Shea came forward to kiss Norah in turn and after inquiring about how the older woman felt Alex bore Niall away to find a vase for the flowers.

'Are you really all right?' Shea asked as they left and Norah nodded.

'I feel wonderful, considering.' She shook her head. 'I don't know why I was so reticent about it.'

Shea smiled. 'I guess that's easy to say in retrospect.'

'I suppose.' Norah frowned slightly. 'Shea, before Alex and Niall return, I want to talk to you. I seem to remember saying something to you before I went into the theatre. About Niall. Did I?'

For one moment Shea felt an urgent need to deny her mother-in-law's hazy memories. And maybe then they could all pretend it never happened. Things would go back to being the same as they had been just short hours ago.

Norah was watching the play of emotions on Shea's face and she sighed resignedly. 'I did, didn't I? I vowed I never would but I suppose it just seemed important to me to get it out into the open, in case anything happened to me.' Her eyes met Shea's.

'How could you have possibly known?' Shea asked softly. 'We...' She swallowed. 'Jamie swore he'd never tell anyone.'

'He didn't tell me.' Norah took hold of Shea's hand where it rested on the bed. 'You remember that dreadful bout of mumps Jamie had when he was about nineteen or twenty? It was one of the severest cases the doctor had seen. He insisted on tests and they found out Jamie was sterile.'

'Sterile?' Shea repeated in shock. 'He didn't tell me that.'

Norah nodded. 'I suspected that. Jamie begged the doctor not to tell anyone but the doctor had discussed the possibility with me before Jamie took the tests. Jamie thought he was the only one who knew about it. I never mentioned it to Jamie because I didn't want to embarrass him.'

'I can't believe—' Shea looked up at Norah. 'When I told Jamie I was pregnant with Niall he said we'd simply let everyone surmise he was Niall's father, that with the family resemblance between Alex and himself no one would suspect the truth. Not even Alex.'

'Why didn't you tell Alex in the beginning, Shea?' Norah asked gently. 'I can't believe Alex would have deserted you and his child. You could have joined him in the States.'

Shea stood up, loath to dredge up the past yet again, but Jamie's mother deserved an explanation.

'I knew how things stood with Alex, Norah. We'd gone through all that before he left. The simple truth was that Alex didn't want me along. And I had no intention of using the fact that I was pregnant to force him to do something he didn't want to do.'

'But—' Norah sighed and shook her head. 'I knew there was something amiss, right from the moment you and Jamie came and told me you were getting married. You'd never had eyes for anyone but Alex. I don't know how many times I wanted to ask you but something always held me back.'

'I was so distraught back then I doubt I would have confided in you, Norah,' Shea said brokenly.

'I sensed all wasn't right with you but Jamie seemed so happy. I didn't want to spoil that. He was my son and as much as I loved Alex—' She shrugged. 'And I've been so guilty over the years. I felt I'd put Jamie's happiness before Alex's. Which I did, didn't I, Shea?'

Shea sat down again and squeezed Norah's hand. 'That's understandable. You shouldn't be ashamed of that. Jamie was a wonderful person.'

'And so is Alex. That's why I wanted you to tell him about Niall. Have you?' she asked the younger woman earnestly, and Shea gave an almost imperceptible nod.

'Alex knows.'

Norah let out the breath she'd obviously been holding. 'And Niall?'

'No. I couldn't... I can't handle that just now, Norah.'
Shea swallowed the lump that threatened to choke her
and pulled herself together. What would Niall think if
he came back and found her in tears? 'But we shouldn't
be talking about this now, Norah. I don't want you
worrying any more than you obviously have been. You
should be concentrating on getting well.'

'Oh, I'm fine. Better than I deserve to be after leading
Dr Robbins a merry dance. But I can't help worrying
about you, Shea. You know I couldn't love you more if
you were my own daughter and I want to see you happy.'

'I know you do, Norah. And I love you, too,' Shea
assured her. 'I am happy. I have you and Niall and my
business. We can work out the rest later.'

'But what about you and Alex? I worry that
you'll—' Norah stopped at the frown on her daughter-
in-law's face. 'Shea, don't hold the past against him.
Alex must have thought at the time that what he was
doing was the best for you.'

Shea bit back a sharp retort. As she saw it Alex had
done what was best for Alex. As Alex had suggested she
had done. The unnerving thought attacked her resolve.

'And we have to think about Niall,' Norah said softly.

Pain ate at Shea again. 'No one could have been a
better father for Niall than Jamie was,' she began, and
Norah nodded.

'I know. But the truth is that we've excluded Alex,
didn't give him the chance to be part of Niall's life.'

Alex had accused her of just that. Shea drove the dis-
quietening thought out of her mind, refusing to acknowledge it. 'Alex was fairly conspicuous by his absence
all these years, wouldn't you say, Norah?' she remarked
dryly, and the older woman was silent for a few moments.

'Feeling the way he did about you, could you honestly
see him coming back here knowing you were Jamie's

wife?' she asked softly before sighing tiredly and resting back against her pillows.

And they were both lost in their own thoughts a few minutes later when Alex and Niall arrived back with the flowers arranged in a large vase.

They stayed with Norah for a little longer before leaving her with the assurances they'd be back the next evening. Niall bounced excitedly between them as they crossed the car park to where Alex had earlier left the Jaguar.

'Can I sit in the front with you, Alex?' he asked excitedly but happily conceded and climbed into the narrow back seat when Alex told him his mother would be more comfortable in the bigger front passenger seat.

She was physically more comfortable, Shea acknowledged, but emotionally she was at sixes and sevens. Sitting this close to Alex played the usual havoc with her senses. So she remained silent on the short journey home, more than content to let Niall carry the conversation with the man next to her.

And they couldn't get home fast enough for Shea. As soon as Alex pulled into the driveway she was out of the car and turning to assist Niall.

'Thanks for seeing us home,' she said quickly, her focus on the third button of Alex's shirt.

'Want some coffee, Alex?' Niall offered easily before Shea could hurry him into the house and she bit back the urge to chastise her son for his good manners.

'Alex is probably tired,' she put in swiftly. 'He'll be wanting to get home.'

'Coffee would be great,' Alex replied just as quickly and Shea could only walk with them up the steps.

That Alex knew she hadn't wanted him to accept Niall's invitation was obvious in the level gaze he bestowed upon her before Niall started for the house.

Silently Shea made the coffee, not attempting to enter the easy dialogue between Niall and his father. She simply wanted to be alone, to plan some course of action to save this intolerable situation. And yet part of her didn't want to face the soul-searching decision-making that she knew solitude would bring.

Niall downed his chocolate milk in record time and gave a blatantly theatrical yawn. 'Gee, I'm pretty tired so I guess I'd better be getting off to bed. I need to be rested for my soccer game tomorrow.'

Shea glanced sharply at him. Usually Niall lobbied to be allowed to stay up later, especially on Friday nights. And with Alex here surely—? She felt her cheeks colour as she suddenly realised he was purposefully leaving her alone with Alex.

Niall came around the table and kissed her on the cheek. ''Night, Mum. See you in the morning, Alex? You won't forget the soccer game, will you?'

Alex assured him he wouldn't and with a grin at them both Niall left them.

A heavy tension grew between them with Niall's exit and Shea made herself stand up, collect the empty mugs.

'I'm a little tired myself,' she said without looking at Alex. 'It's been quite a day, what with Norah being rushed to hospital and all. I think I'll have an early night, too.'

'I need an answer, Shea,' he said softly, and Shea's heartbeats raced in her chest.

She desperately wanted to plead ignorance of his meaning but she knew that would only prolong her agony. With outward calm she rinsed the crockery.

'I can't marry you, Alex. You must see that,' she said evenly.

CHAPTER TWELVE

'No, I don't.' He was standing now, and had moved around the table. 'We were always meant for each other. *You* must see that,' he mimicked her ironically.

'I'm tired of telling you I like my life the way it is, Alex.'

'And I can only repeat, what about Niall's life?'

'There's nothing wrong with the way I'm bringing up my son. He's happy and he's healthy. That's all I'm interested in.'

'He needs a father. Why not me?'

'And I could say, why you, Alex?' Shea said through clenched teeth. 'Good grief! I haven't seen you for eleven years. And apart from that, there are plenty of nice guys around here if I'd felt the need at any time since Jamie died to provide Niall with a father.'

'Like that real estate guy?' Alex cut in scathingly.

Shea shut the door of the dishwasher with controlled anger. 'I'm not going to argue with you about this, Alex. The subject is closed as far as I'm concerned.'

'Closed?' He gave a soft, mocking laugh. 'It will never be closed, Shea. Not tonight. Or the night after that. We opened the door on it the day we met.'

He moved closer to her and she caught the scent of his body, the musky odour of his aftershave, the aroma that was purely his. And it was as familiar to her as her own. Memories of it, the smell, the taste, the feel of him, began to weave a web of wanting about her.

'The years between mean nothing,' he continued lowly. 'You know that as well as I do.'

'Alex, please.' Her hand went out unconsciously to ward him off and she swallowed, her mouth dry as her body heated up. 'Must we discuss this now? I'm tired and I—'

He caught her hand gently in his, slowly brought her fingers to the warmth of his lips, his tongue tip teasing each fingertip in turn. And Shea's body surged on a wave of desire. How she wished—

And then his lips touched hers, feather-soft kisses challenging the iron control she told herself she possessed. He moved his mouth slightly away from her and she couldn't prevent her own from following. She knew she was asking him, begging him to kiss her again, yet she couldn't seem to prevent that almost imperceptible movement that surely betrayed her.

Alex drew her body forward until it rested against his and only then did his lips reclaim hers, his tongue intimately caressing. Shea felt as though her insides were melting and a small part of her screamed for her to stop this now, before she was totally incapable of doing so.

A low moan escaped from her and she pushed desperately against his chest. Alex allowed her to lean away from him but held her fast, his lower body still moulded to hers. His eyes were dark chocolate-brown pools, and she wasn't left in any doubt that he was as inflamed as she was.

'Let me go, Alex. I don't want to do this.' Her face flushed again at the deliberate untruths and the faint twisting of his lips told her he knew she was lying.

'I can tell that you don't,' he said sardonically, his husky tone also revealing his own arousal, his eyes touching on the swell of her breasts against her blouse.

'Niall's in the next room,' Shea said desperately. 'He could come in and see—'

'He hasn't seen you kiss a man before?'

'No, he hasn't. Only his fath—' Shea's voice died on the words and Alex's mouth twisted again. 'Only Jamie,' Shea corrected, and this time Alex did thrust her from him.

He turned away, one hand going to massage the back of his neck.

She knew she had cut him with her words and suddenly she wished she could draw them back.

'Look, I'm sorry,' Shea began, and he swung back to face her.

'I'm sure you are,' he said harshly and then swore under his breath. 'I still can't believe Jamie was part of this, this charade you lived. I can't believe he'd do it to me.'

'To you?' Shea shook her head wearily. 'He didn't do it to you, Alex. He did it for me.' Her words hung heavily in the room and then Alex sighed and gave a slight nod.

'Yes. I guess he did.' His eyes held hers, seemed to burn down into her very soul, stirred up a churning mass of memories she'd fought so long to subdue. 'Jamie would have done anything for you,' Alex continued flatly. 'So would I. It was always that way from the moment we both saw you.' He paused. 'Goodnight, Shea,' he said softly as he left her.

The next morning Shea dragged herself out of bed in time to open the shop. That Niall was up and ready to attend his soccer fixture, his eyes alight with the knowledge that Alex would be there to see him play, did nothing to improve Shea's ill humour. But after the mechanic had fixed her car she dutifully kissed her son goodbye and wished him luck with his game.

And she was still no closer to deciding what she was going to do about the problem of Alex. His outrageous proposal had kept filtering into her mind at every opportunity during her sleepless night. It continued to taunt her as a hectic influx of weekend customers entered the shop.

She'd refused to marry him, she told herself for the hundredth time. So what was the point wasting time and energy examining it over and over again? How she wished she could—

It was only natural that a small part of her would want to forget the past and accept his offer of marriage, she continued to tell herself, grimacing wryly. Hadn't being married to Alex Finlay been all she'd ever wanted from the moment she'd first set eyes on him? Until he'd so easily walked away from her when she'd needed him the most.

Her anger at Alex had been part of her life for so long, she couldn't deny that, but was she capable of putting so much pain behind her? Could she, for Niall's sake if not for her own?

During the first lull of the afternoon Shea poured herself a cup of coffee and relaxed back against the counter. She almost groaned when the door opened again.

'Shea!' David greeted her with a smile. 'I came straight over. This almost calls for a celebration. Don't you think so?'

'A celebration?' Shea frowned.

'You mean Finlay hasn't been in touch with you? I took it that he had. I've just had him on the phone and he's agreed to the lease. And with great terms.'

'Alex agreed—?'

David nodded. 'I can't believe he hasn't contacted you himself. The terms are more than reasonable and well within your budget.' David adjusted the knot of his tie. 'Actually, they're far better than I expected. Of course it took a good bit of negotiation,' he added, one hand self-satisfiedly smoothing his hair. He leant across and quietly mentioned a figure.

Shea set her coffee mug carefully on the counter. What was Alex playing at? He'd refused to make any commitment about the lease and now he was handing it to her on a platter.

'In my opinion,' David beamed, 'you should snap it up, Shea, before he changes his mind. The building's ready for immediate occupancy. You can start anytime getting it fitted out to suit you.'

'I thought he'd be asking at least half as much again,' she said quietly and looked levelly at the other man. 'Are there any strings attached?' she asked sharply, and David's eyebrows wavered in surprise.

'No. What sort of strings?'

Shea shrugged. 'I don't know. It just seems too good to be true, that's all.'

'Of course, as you know, Shea, our agency uses the accepted contracts and agreements. They're all above-board and—'

'I didn't mean legal strings,' Shea reassured him quickly. 'I guess I just meant, well, were there any unusual stipulations or. . .' Her words dwindled away.

How could she put into words the quivering sensation she felt in the pit of her stomach as her sudden suspicion took root and began to grow inside her? Did Alex's unexpected benevolence have anything to do with his discovery that Niall was his son? Or with his subsequent marriage proposal?

'No. No added clauses of any kind,' David told her. 'Finlay agreed with me it was advantageous to have one building occupied as soon as possible to encourage other businesses to take up the rest of the estate. Sensible really.' David shrugged. 'I can't honestly say I like the guy much but I'd say he's being extremely fair with this.'

Shea tuned out as the so familiar voice inside her asked her if Alex was to be trusted. Were his motives as altruistic as David seemed to think they were? Shea rather doubted it. And the only way she could find out was to ask Alex himself. She dragged her thoughts back to David.

'And I wondered if you'd care to go? To the beach concert tomorrow night,' he added when Shea blinked at him bewilderedly.

Shea almost laughed. David was asking her out. Now. When Alex had made his inconceivable proposal.

She should go with David, show Alex he couldn't call all the shots. The defiant thought died as quickly as it had been born. David Aston was a nice person and she couldn't use him that way.

Shea gently declined his invitation, explaining she would be tied up visiting Norah at the hospital, and he accepted her refusal equitably enough. And after he'd left, assuring her he'd have the lease papers ready by Monday, Shea wondered again why she couldn't consider David as a prospective partner.

Because Alex had spoiled her for any other man, stated that direct, unsympathetic voice inside her.

The thought continued to gnaw at her. And even as she tried to deny it again, she knew it was true. She'd never been interested in anyone else. Only Alex. Even Jamie hadn't reached the depths of her very soul the way Alex had.

Time dragged by, the rush of morning customers tapering off markedly as the afternoon wore on. So when the door opened Shea glanced up eagerly, hoping another customer would at least make the half hour before closing time pass more quickly.

'Hello, Shea.'

The welcoming smile died on her face even as her traitorous heartbeats played a bizarre tattoo in her breast at the sight of him. What was Alex doing here? Come to gloat? Or to call in his marker for granting her the lease on the building?

Although she'd all but decided she was going to seek him out and ask him about the lease, she'd wanted it to be in her own time, on her terms.

She glanced at her wristwatch. 'I'll be closing soon,' she said quickly.

'I know. I've just been to see Norah. She said I should catch you before you left.'

'If you've come here to tell me the good news about the lease, I already know. David was here earlier. He told me about it.' Shea paused. 'What I'm unsure about is the reason why you changed your mind so suddenly.'

'I didn't. I simply came to a decision.'

Shea's hands grasped the edge of the counter for support. 'I know what you're doing, Alex, and it won't work. I'd rather settle on another building. I won't let you manipulate me with that lease.'

'Manipulate you?' Alex's eyes narrowed. 'In what way?'

Shea gave an exclamation of exasperation and his head went up.

'As in do as I ask or I won't give you the lease,' he bit out sharply, glaring at her.

'I see it more as, I've given you the lease on such wonderful terms, now it's your turn to do me a little favour.'

'Like marrying me?' Alex said quietly, and Shea swallowed.

In bald facts said aloud it sounded cold and ugly. And so far-reached from the Alex she had once known that Shea felt a burning ache in her chest, and tears stung her eyes.

Alex gave a soft, harsh laugh. 'I think perhaps you were right, Shea, when you said eleven years was a long time, that people change. Maybe I haven't moved with the times. As far as I was concerned marriage used to go hand in hand with love. For me it still does.'

Shea's throat closed as pain rose to choke her. What right had Alex to talk about love?

'That's another problem of mine, you see,' Alex continued flatly. 'I tried to stop loving you and I haven't had a lot of success to date. But it had nothing to do with any bloody factory building.' His eyes held hers and then he sighed.

'Take the lease, Shea. In the manner that it's given. In the interests of good business practice. Or leave it. Get Aston to let me know your decision.' He turned abruptly and walked out, letting the door close quietly behind him.

Shea glanced again at her wristwatch and walked across to the open door of the huge warehouse. It wasn't like Bill Denham to be unreliable. She'd used his carpentry skills on some renovations to her first factory and had always found him competent and punctual. Which was why she was surprised he was over fifteen minutes late.

She unfolded the rough sketches she'd made of her plan to shop fit the new factory and checked a few of her measurements, ready to discuss them with the carpenter.

But of course her attention wandered again, as it had been doing quite regularly since the weekend. Since those moments in the shop before Alex had walked away. And she'd let him go.

Shea sighed and ran a hand through her loose hair. This morning she'd been too tired to clip it back in its usual chignon and she felt pale and unflatteringly jaded.

A rusting utility truck pulled to a halt by the open door and Bill Denham sprang from the cab and hurried towards Shea.

'Sorry I'm late, Shea,' he said as he joined her, pulling off his battered cap and shoving it into his hip pocket. 'I was on my way back from Mullumbimby and had to make a detour. There's some sort of pile-up on the road into town so I had to take the long way 'round. Along with everyone else,' he added with a shrug.

'Oh, dear.' Shea frowned. 'I hope no one was badly hurt.'

'Looked pretty awful, what with all the smoke. I caught a newsflash on the radio about it. Sounds like a petrol tanker jack-knifed and clipped a car and a bus. That's all they said, apart from advising everyone to give it a wide berth. There's quite a traffic jam.'

'Did you say a bus was involved?' Shea asked, a wave of dread washing over her. 'How long ago did it happen?'

Bill shrugged. 'Not sure. Half to three-quarters of an hour at a guess.'

Shea swallowed a rush of panic. She'd thought she'd heard sirens as she'd turned off the highway but they'd been up ahead of her and she hadn't given them a thought.

'It wasn't a school bus, was it?' she asked softly, and Bill scratched his greying hair.

'Bit early for the school bus, isn't it?'

'My son's school soccer team was playing in Ballina today. I—' Shea's stomach clenched with anxiety and she swallowed. 'Look, Bill, I'll have to go. I'll have to check that Niall's not involved. I'm sorry. I'll ring you.'

Before the man had time to comment Shea had thrust the sketches for the alterations into his hands and was out the door and climbing into her car.

Please God, don't let Niall be involved in the accident. She kept repeating the words to herself like a litany as she sped along the outbound road. She didn't have far to go before she came upon the backup of traffic, the police busily detouring them along a side-road. Agitatedly she pulled her car off onto the shoulder and ran towards the blockade of police cars.

The acrid smell of petroleum and smoke hung in the air, making her throat tighten. She didn't know the policeman directing cars onto the side-road but she recognised the officer standing by a police car, talking into a radio handpiece. He put down the microphone as Shea rushed up to him.

'Rick! The bus that was involved in the accident, was it the school bus?' she asked breathlessly, and the policeman reached out a hand to steady her.

'The boys are fine, Shea,' he began, and Shea clutched at the car for support.

'It was Niall's school bus? Oh, no.'

'None of the boys are hurt,' the young policeman assured her. 'Just a bit shaken up.'

'I have to go down there. Can you let my car through?'

'Hop into the patrol car and I'll drive you down.'

Shea thanked him as he helped her into the passenger seat.

He waved to the other officers as he manoeuvered the patrol car past the roadblock and when they rounded the curve in the road Shea gasped in horror.

Red and blue lights flashed everywhere and behind it all the overturned tanker lay on its side covered in foam, the grass and trees around it blackened by fire.

But Shea barely registered the scene as she searched for the yellow school bus Niall's soccer team would have been travelling in and her hands clenched together when she saw it. The bus had obviously left the road and ploughed through long grass, coming to a halt, nose into a clump of scrubby trees.

The boys were standing in a group some distance away watching the fire fighters deal with the huge truck and its ruptured fuel tank.

'Hard to believe no one was killed, isn't it?' the policeman said as he stopped the car. 'If the tanker had been full of petrol it might have been another story. The driver got out with a sprained ankle and singed eye-brows and the woman driver of the car over there has a suspected broken arm. Luckily none of the boys got so much as a scratch although the bus driver—'

Shea barely heard him as she jumped out of the car and ran towards the group of boys. She almost moaned with relief as she spotted Niall's fair head. He was standing with Pete and when he saw her he gave her a surprised grin. Shea threw her arms around him and hugged him to her.

'What are you doing here, Mum?' Niall asked as she released him. 'Did the police go and get you?'

'I heard about the accident and I thought—' Shea stopped and hugged him again.

'Mum!' Niall protested softly. 'I'm OK. Really. But I won't be if you keep squeezing me so hard.'

Shea laughed brokenly and she had to stop herself clutching her son to her again. Instead she turned to the other boys. 'What about the rest of you? Are you all right, Pete?'

Niall's best friend nodded. 'Sure, Mrs Finlay. But it was a bit scary. You should have seen the tanker go up. It was awesome.'

The other boys agreed.

'Coach had to swing the bus around that car over there,' continued one of the other boys. 'And then we ran off the road. Like in the movies.'

'We all had to climb out the back emergency window,' Niall told her. 'Alex broke it in.'

CHAPTER THIRTEEN

SHEA turned back to her son in surprise. 'Alex? Alex was here?'

Niall nodded. 'In the bus. He came with us to see the game.'

'I didn't know—' Shea paused. 'Where... Where is he now?'

'In the ambulance,' Niall replied.

'In the—' Shea's lips seemed to have gone numb and she had trouble forming her words. She thought seeing Niall safe and unhurt would have put an end to her shock but suddenly her stomach was plummeting wildly again. 'Was he hurt?' she asked as casually as she could.

'He had blood all over his shirt,' Pete put in with relish, and Shea felt herself pale.

'Stay here,' she said firmly. 'I won't— I'll just—'

She took a couple of slow steps and then began to run over to where two ambulances were parked. Yet she seemed to get there in slow motion.

Her heart was beating like a drum. Alex was hurt? How badly? What if—? She had a pain in her chest, felt as though something inside her was breaking. All her muscles seemed to have turned to water as she forced herself to walk around to the open door at the back of the first vehicle.

There was a man lying on one of the stretchers. He had a bandage around his head and when Shea looked closer she recognised the pale face of Niall's soccer coach.

Alex was sitting on the other stretcher, quietly talking to the coach. As Pete had said, his shirt was liberally splattered with blood and Shea grabbed at the open door of the ambulance for support as her legs threatened to give way beneath her.

She must have made some sound for Alex's gaze turned to her and their eyes met, held for long seconds before Shea swallowed the hard lump in her throat.

'Are you all right?' she asked him as calmly as she could, and he held up his bandaged arm.

'I'm fine. Just a few scratches.' He continued to hold her gaze and Shea was aware of a loud roaring in her ears.

She made herself look away, over to the coach, and she dazedly inquired after him.

'Hit my head, so I was lucky. It's the hardest part of me,' he laughed weakly.

'Have you seen Niall?' Alex asked. 'He's not hurt.'

Shea nodded. 'He told me you were here.'

All sorts of jumbled emotions seemed to be making peculiar patterns in the smoke-filled air between them and Shea's fingers turned white where she still clasped the door. She wanted to throw herself into his arms, hold him to her in relief, the way she'd just done to Niall. And yet not quite the same way.

At that moment the ambulance man joined her. 'We have to head off now,' he gently told Shea, and she stepped back.

'I—' Shea swallowed again. 'Will you be OK?' she asked Alex lamely, and he nodded.

The ambulance officer closed the doors and Shea stood and watched the vehicle drive away. For long minutes she continued to stand there before she drew herself together and walked back to the waiting boys.

'Did they fix up the cut on Alex's arm?' Niall asked her, and she nodded.

'He's gone to the hospital with your coach but they both seemed all right.'

All right. What mundane words to use in such a situation, Shea reflected wryly. All right. Now that she had seen the extent of Alex's injuries she could perhaps say that she was all right, too. With a sinking feeling she somehow rather doubted if she would ever be all right again.

'What a lucky escape,' Norah repeated as they cleared away the dishes after dinner. She had been out of hospital for just one day and seemed none the worse for her own ordeal. 'I heard the report of the accident on the radio but I never dreamed Niall and Alex would be involved.'

'Yes,' Shea agreed carefully.

'One of the guys said it was just like in the movies,' Niall remarked. 'But it wasn't. It's a lot different being in the middle of it than it is watching it on the screen.' He gave a lopsided grin that reminded Shea of Alex. 'I think I prefer watching it on the screen.'

'And Alex had to break the emergency window to get you all out of the bus?' Norah questioned Niall, although he had already told her in great detail about the accident, Alex's part in it featuring strongly.

'That's how he cut his arm and there was blood all over his shirt.' Niall seemed to be getting as much pleasure from reporting this fact as his friend, Pete, had. 'It was gruesome.'

Norah looked across at her daughter-in-law. 'If Alex has a cut arm perhaps he'll be finding it difficult to make his meal.'

Niall frowned. 'Gran's right, Mum. Do you think we should check how he is? We could take him some of Gran's soup. We have plenty left over.'

'I'm sure Alex will be all right,' Shea began. All right. The two insipid words were plaguing her.

'What if he isn't?' Niall persisted. 'What if he's really hungry?'

'Why don't you just slip over and see, Shea?' Norah added her appeal to Niall's.

Shea glanced at the container of soup and then across to her mother-in-law. If Alex's wounds weren't as superficial as he'd implied— 'I guess it wouldn't hurt to drive over, with the soup,' she said softly. 'Perhaps Niall could come, too.'

Niall glanced at his grandmother. 'I think I'd better stay here with Gran, seeing as she's just out of hospital,' he said quickly. 'It wouldn't take you long, Mum.'

'No. I suppose it wouldn't.' Shea stood up uncertainly.

'Actually, Gran and I will be fine so take as long as you like,' Niall added.

Shea glanced at him sharply and he gave her a guileless look.

'Tell Alex we said hello,' Norah said then. 'And that we hope his arm is better soon.'

Shea nodded and picked up the container of soup. For a moment she'd suspected her son and her mother-in-law of some sort of conspiracy but she reluctantly rejected the idea, deciding she was being paranoid.

She was wearing a pair of tailored shorts and a light T-shirt and as she walked out into the hall she considered changing her clothes. But if she did she knew she might lose her nerve and not go at all, so she continued on out to the car.

During the short drive Shea couldn't quite focus her thoughts. She wanted to plan what she'd say to Alex when she saw him but she couldn't seem to concentrate. Her mind kept flashing images from the past.

A young Alex with his long, unruly sun-bleached hair the first time she'd seen him. Alex in his dirt-and-grass-stained football jersey accepting a winning trophy. Her sixteenth birthday and the feel of his lips when he'd kissed her. And the first time they'd made love.

A lump rose in her throat. How she'd loved him. Still loved him.

A few lights blazed in the lower floor windows of Alex's house as she turned through the gates and drove slowly up the driveway. She switched off the ignition and sat there for long moments, undecided now about whether she should have come.

She was as attracted to him as she'd ever been and she knew that would never change. It would be that way no matter what happened.

She'd held him at arm's length since his return because she thought she hated him for what he'd done. Yet from the moment he'd walked into that town meeting she'd known she had been deluding herself. She'd told herself so often over the years that he meant nothing to her that she thought she believed it.

But could she trust him not to hurt her again?

He'd asked her to marry him, she reminded herself. So he could be part of Niall's life, she added, torturing herself again. Yet part of her wanted to accept his proposal, on whatever terms he offered.

That particular thought unsettled her so much she was out of the car and ringing the doorbell before she realised she was doing it.

The sound echoed inside the house but no one answered the door. She rang the bell again with the same result.

What if there'd been some sort of complication with Alex's wound and they'd decided to keep him in hospital? What if—? Shea pulled herself together. If Alex was still at the hospital there would hardly be lights on in the house.

She reached out and tried the doorknob and it turned in her hands. Tentatively she opened the door and called out his name. There was no reply.

What if he was suffering from some sort of delayed shock? Shea walked inside, calling his name. She checked the study and the kitchen. Leaving the container of soup on the table, she returned to the hall. A low light burned out on the patio and she realised the sliding-glass doors were open.

He was standing on the edge of the tiled courtyard, his back to her, looking out towards the bay. The muffled roar of the surf pounding on the sand throbbed on the still air.

'Alex?'

At the sound of her voice he turned his head.

'I rang the bell but you mustn't have heard me.'

His face was in shadow so she couldn't see his expression but her eyes took in the familiar shape of him, vaguely backlit by the low garden lighting.

Then he stepped forward and in the light from the open doors she saw he was bare chested and wore only a pair of faded cut-off jeans.

'I came to...' Shea swallowed. 'I brought you some of Norah's homemade soup. We thought you might have had trouble cooking. I mean, with your arm and...' Her voice gave out on her.

'I managed with some leftovers. But thanks.'

Shea cleared her throat. 'Well. That's OK.'

The night air thickened as they stood looking at each other.

Shea dragged her eyes from him. 'I guess I should be going then. Norah and Niall will be wondering why I'm taking so long.' She realised what could be read between the lines of what she'd said and she flushed. 'Um. Goodbye, then.'

She turned slowly and made herself walk towards the door.

'Shea.'

She stopped but couldn't look back at him and she heard him sigh.

'Thanks,' he said flatly. 'For bringing the soup. For coming.'

The edge of dejection, almost defeat, in his voice cut into her and the tears she'd been holding in check overflowed, began to course down her cheeks.

'I meant it, Shea.' He'd walked up behind her and she felt the faint shift of her hair from his breath.

Defensively she moved her head forward so that her hair shielded her face. She didn't want him to see her crying.

'I know it must have been difficult for you to come. I haven't exactly endeared myself to you these past couple of weeks and—'

'I didn't really come to bring you the soup.' The words echoed inside her head and she stiffened, not knowing if she'd said them.

'Why did you come then?' His softly spoken query answered her question.

'I came because—' Shea swallowed and surreptitiously wiped her cheek with her hand.

'Because?'

'I...I was worried about you.' She moved forward, took a couple of steps through the doorway, then turned to face him. But he was still far too close to her, and suddenly she didn't quite know where to put her hands. They yearned to reach for him but she clasped them together in front of her.

Alex had moved into the doorway and stood, to all outward appearances, casually leaning against the door jamb.

Almost mesmerised, Shea's eyes went to the clean white bandage on his forearm, and then to the tanned skin of his bare chest, and slipped lower. She swallowed convulsively as she realised that the stud at the waist of his cut-off jeans was undone, that the material clung to him, riding low on his hips. She wanted nothing more than to lean forward and kiss the firm flesh of his flat stomach. And her heartbeats renewed their thundering, covetous rhythm.

Her eyes rose to meet his. 'I couldn't believe that you would leave me,' she heard herself say brokenly. The words she had no intention of saying held the remembered pain of all those years ago and Alex paled, his knuckles whitening where his fingers clung to the doorframe.

'It very nearly killed me to do it,' he said thickly. 'I honestly thought I was doing the right thing. The noble thing. Giving you time to grow up. Furthering my education so I'd be in a better position to provide for you.' He swallowed and she watched the muscles of his neck move beneath his skin. 'I wanted—' He shook his head and a strand of hair fell forward over his brow.

'In retrospect I can't believe my arrogance. I was so sure of how I thought you felt about me it never occurred to me that you could find someone else. I thought in a year or two I'd come back and we'd pick up where we'd left off. I never so much as suspected you were pregnant. And the very last thing I wanted to do was to hurt you, Shea.'

'I couldn't, I still can't understand why you didn't discuss your plans to go with Joe Rosten with me,' Shea said. 'When you just sprang it on me I think I must have gone into shock.'

'In the beginning I fully intended taking you with me but my father and Joe said perhaps that wouldn't be fair on you. I could see that. And it's not an excuse. I thought

I'd be asking you to give up your life, your aspirations, to live mine.'

'I would have done that, Alex.'

'I know you would have. I didn't think I had the right to ask you to.' He sighed. 'I wish so much now that I had.'

Neither of them spoke and the air between them was charged with heightened emotion again.

'Can you possibly forgive me?' he asked at last.

'Eleven years ago I vowed I never would,' Shea said softly. 'But today when Niall said you were in the ambulance and I thought, well—' Shea drew a steadying breath. 'I realised how easy it would have been for me to have left telling you how I felt until it was too late. Again. So—'

Shea pulled at the hem of her T-shirt. 'You were right, Alex. I let my anger at you for going and my guilt because I knew I was giving Jamie second best to ferment inside me all these years. When you turned up out of the blue I couldn't handle the fact that I only had to see you to fall in love with you all over again.'

She took a tentative step towards him. 'I love you, Alex,' she said simply. 'I always have. From the moment I saw you when I was twelve years old.'

'Shea.' Her name broke from him and his arms slowly reached out for her. Tenderly he drew her against him and Shea melted into him as she heard him sigh.

'I loved you, too. More than life itself.' He held her gaze. 'That hasn't changed, either. I still do.'

He ran his hands up her arms, moved his fingers into her hair, held her head so that he could rain light urgent kisses on her brow, her eyes, her nose, and then her lips. With a low moan he crushed her to him and they clung together. When they eventually pulled apart they were both breathless.

'I don't know about you, but I need to sit down,' Alex said softly and led her back across the courtyard. He lowered himself onto the soft cushions of a large patio chair, pulling her down beside him so that she was almost lying on top of him. 'My God! I can't believe you're here in my arms,' he said huskily and kissed her again.

'Eleven long, wasted years,' he murmured against her mouth. 'If only I could turn back the clock.' He looked deeply into her eyes. 'I've made a complete mess of everything I've touched since I left you.'

'That can't be true,' she said. 'I mean, this house, your other properties—'

'Material things don't count, Shea, believe me. I meant, if I could only change things at least then I wouldn't have hurt so many people. You. Patti. It seems my decision to leave Byron Bay started a chain reaction of hurt for everyone around me.

'And every time I tried to make amends I only made things worse. I just about went to pieces when I heard you'd married Jamie. I walked around like a robot for months. And when Jamie wrote and said you'd had a son, well, I felt as though someone had cut out my heart.'

'I never knew Jamie wrote to you. He didn't tell me. But I suppose he couldn't.'

Alex sighed against her hair. 'I decided if you could marry Jamie so quickly you couldn't have loved me very much. So I married Patti because you were lost to me. Another terrible mistake.'

'I also thought Patti Rosten was part of the reason why you left,' Shea told him, and Alex shook his head.

'There was never anyone but you. But back then I did honestly believe I could make a go of my marriage. Patti said she loved me and I thought I could help her with her problems, the alcohol and the drugs. Once again I only seemed to compound the problem. Our marriage was over before the year was out.

'So when I heard about Jamie's death I thought, enough. I knew I had to come home to you. That's when Patti took an overdose. Her father was away and she was alone. I had to stay with her. She said she wanted to try again to make our marriage work and Joe begged me to give it a go.

'I knew I owed it to Patti.' He sighed again. 'It took some time but between us Joe and I convinced Patti to get help. She met Nick, the guy she married, at the clinic. So everything ended up happily for her.'

His fingers played with a strand of her hair. 'So I thought it was time I tried for my own happily ever after. Joe let me cut down on my workload for him, I re-arranged my schedules with the business, and I set off.'

Alex grimaced wryly. 'And when I finally got here you let me know you weren't exactly ecstatic to see me and I thought I'd waited too long.'

'Oh, Alex. I'm sorry.' Shea buried her face in the light matt of hair on his chest, breathing in the heady scent of him. Then she looked up. 'I should have—'

Alex put a finger over her lips. 'I don't blame you for giving me the short shift.' He shook his head. 'If I'd known I was leaving you to have a child alone—' He ran his finger along the line of her jaw. 'I thought we were being so careful.'

'I couldn't believe it, either. I was terrified and exalted all at the one time. I guess I didn't even consider that we wouldn't just get married and have our baby. Looking back I was excruciatingly naïve. I was going to tell you that night you said you were leaving. You sounded so distant, so cold.'

'Oh, Shea. It was all front. I knew you'd be upset but I thought if I was offhand, matter-of-fact— God, Shea, what a mess I made of everything.'

'We made of everything,' she corrected him softly. 'But one very good thing came out of it. Niall. I've never regretted having him, not for a moment. He kept me sane in the early days. And Jamie. Poor Jamie. I guess I'll always feel I short-changed him. He knew I didn't love him, not the way I loved you, and he deserved someone who loved him that way. I told him that but he wanted to marry me anyway.' Shea looked up at him. 'Do you think we can put all this behind us, Alex?'

'I know we can,' Alex said with feeling.

'We'll have to explain all this to Niall—'

'We'll do it together when the time's right.' He looked down at her. 'You know, Niall has your eyes. When he looked up at me that first night I nearly fell apart.'

'You said he could have been your son.'

'In my wildest dreams I never imagined that he was.'

Shea wiped a tear from her face. 'He's very like you. When he smiles at me, I see you.'

Alex brushed a thumb against her cheek, caught a tear and brought it to his lips. 'I'm not making the same mistake twice you know. I'm getting you to the altar before you can change your mind.'

Shea laughed softly through her tears. 'Is that what you call a proposal?'

'I propose to try to be as good a father to Niall as Jamie was. And I propose to love you for the rest of our lives. Any improvement?' he asked lightly.

'A little.' She ran her fingers lightly over his chest, down his flat midriff, fiddled with the open stud on his cut-offs, and he made a low purring noise deep in his throat.

He moved then, setting her back on the cushions of the chair before kneeling beside her. 'Will you marry me, Shea?'

'I will,' she said seriously, and he lowered his head, kissing her as only Alex could.

Her fingers retraced their steps and the rasp of his zipper seemed to momentarily drown out the sound of the surf, the soft whisper of the swaying palm fronds overhead.

Alex's lips left hers, trailed downwards over her chin, settled seductively in the V of her neckline, his tongue tip tasting her skin. His hands slid beneath her T-shirt, lifted it over her head, and he unclipped her bra. With a low moan his lips continued their journey until she writhed beneath him.

He stood up and quickly removed his shorts and the dim light momentarily caught the hard contours of him as he stood before her. And Shea's body ached with desire.

Her world fell silently back into place.

'Alex,' she whispered huskily. 'Make love to me.'

Then his strong, tanned body loomed over her, shutting out the shaft of moonlight that had been dancing between the rustling leaves above them, the light salty breeze playing along their naked bodies . . .

HARLEQUIN PRESENTS®

Follow your heart, not your head,
in our exciting series:

—when passion knows no reason...

Watch for these dramatic stories about women who
know the odds are against them—
but take the risk all the same!

Dare to love in:

**June 1997—HIS COUSIN'S WIFE (#1891)
by Lynsey Stevens
July 1997—WHISPER OF SCANDAL (#1898)
by Kathryn Ross**

Available wherever Harlequin books are sold.

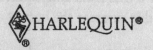

He changes diapers, mixes formula and
tells wonderful bedtime stories—he's

Mr. Mom

Three totally different stories of sexy, single
heroes each raising another man's child...
from three of your favorite authors:

MEMORIES OF THE PAST
by Carole Mortimer

THE MARRIAGE TICKET
by Sharon Brondos

TELL ME A STORY
by Dallas Schulze

Available this June wherever
Harlequin and Silhouette books are sold.

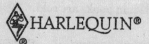

HARLEQUIN® Silhouette®

HARLEQUIN ◇ PRESENTS®

Don't miss these fun-filled romances that feature
fantastic men who *eventually* make fabulous fathers.
Ready or not...

Watch for:

June 1997—FINN'S TWINS! (#1890)
by Anne McAllister
July 1997—THE DADDY DEAL (#1897)
by Kathleen O'Brien

FROM HERE TO PATERNITY—
men who find their way to fatherhood
by fair means, by foul, or even by default!

Available wherever Harlequin books are sold.